IN THE
SHADOWS

Text story by
KIERSTEN WHITE

Art and art story by
JIM DI BARTOLO
Based upon an original story
concept by Jim Di Bartolo

SCHOLASTIC PRESS

Story (art and text) compilation copyright © 2014
by Jim Di Bartolo and Kiersten Brazier

Artwork copyright © 2014 by Jim Di Bartolo
Text copyright © 2014 by Kiersten Brazier

Library of Congress Cataloging-in-Publication Data
Available

ISBN 978-0-545-56144-0

10 9 8 7 6 5 4 3 2 1   14 15 16 17 18
Printed in Singapore 46

First edition, May 2014

The text type was set in Adobe Garamond Pro.
Book design by Christopher Stengel

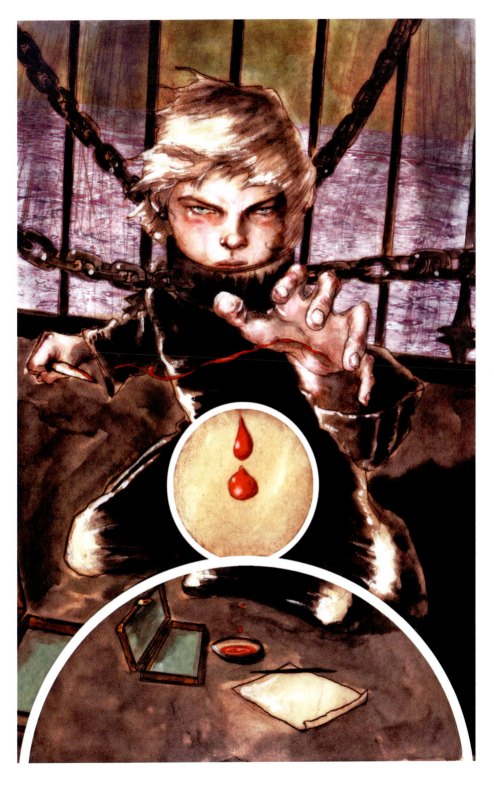

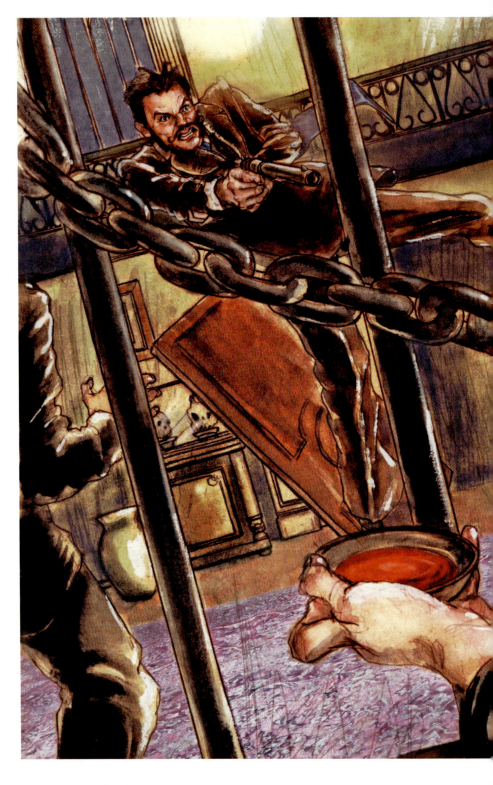

ONE

THE WORLD SWAYED BENEATH CORA. She leaned her cheek against the tree's rough bark, overcome with a dizzy wash of vertigo that wasn't entirely unpleasant.

She was in the witch's tree.

Taking a deep breath, she pulled herself higher through the branches. When her straw hat got in her way, she tossed it toward the ground to wait beside her shoes, stockings, and garters. Once she'd gone as far as she safely could, she wrapped an arm around the trunk and leaned out, letting the sun play on her face between the broad oak leaves. The smell of green overpowered the heavy salt scent of the ocean, and she could just make out the cross from the church and the distant top of the lighthouse.

Minnie and the O'Connell boys hovered at the bottom of the hill, afraid to even set foot on the line that marked the witch's property. Cora was fifteen, far too old for climbing trees, but now she had done something her sister never would. Their summer-long series of dares had escalated to this, and Cora knew she'd won. She waved a hand and crowed wildly, flush with her own triumph.

In response, Minnie's face went white with terror, and the boys yelped and turned tail, fleeing into the woods.

Cora slowly turned her head. She'd come level with the second story of the house, where a single round window looked out like a dark eye.

The witch was standing behind it, staring right at her. Pale face expressionless, she raised a hand and put it against the glass, fingers splayed wide.

At that very same moment, a bird flung itself at Cora, a cacophony of feathers and screeching. As she raised her hands to protect her face, Cora's feet lost their hold.

Before she realized she was falling, everything went black.

Cora awoke to blinding pain, contrasted by a cool hand at her forehead.

A sweet voice hummed an off-key tune, and Cora peeled her eyes open to see a dim, curtained room lit by pillared candles. The walls were lined with stacks and stacks of books, so many that she couldn't make out the pattern on the wallpaper behind them.

She was lying on a stiff sofa. Next to her was a woman, hair dark around her face but gradually lightening to blond at the end of a braid draped across her knees with the sleek twist of a snake. She wore merely a slip, no corset or stays or even drawers. A necklace with a dark green beetle charm nestled in the sharp hollow of her collarbone. The woman's eyes drifted down and then locked onto Cora's. A heartbeat too late, Cora thought to squeeze them shut again and play at being asleep. Sleep had been safe.

Once caught, Cora could not look away from the black depths of the witch's eyes. She was in the Witch of Barley Hill's house. No one — *no one* — had ever been inside.

The witch smiled, but it was disconnected, like her mouth and eyes had forgotten how to speak to each other. "Hello, little bird. You fell out of your nest."

"I'm sorry," Cora whispered. "Please don't hurt me."

"You don't need me for that, do you?" The witch's grin widened to reveal teeth that looked impossibly old and yellowed in her unlined face. "People are very good at hurting themselves. I never have to do a thing." She held up her fingers, which were dark with something.

Blood.

Screaming, Cora scrambled back along the sofa, falling heavily to the floor and knocking over a stack of books in an avalanche of dust and paper. As she lunged up and ran for the door, the witch's voice came soft but inescapable behind her.

"No need to fear death, my dear. It's already at your door. Better to be caught than to run forever."

Cora's sweat-slick hands fumbled, finally turning the doorknob. She fled into the sunshine, the cold sorrow of the witch's voice clinging to her shoulders. Minnie, a knife clutched in her hand, was already halfway up the walk.

"Go!" Cora yelled, and, arms wrapped around each other, they stumbled back home, breathless and weeping with terror.

The next morning their father was dead.

TWO

THE CASE IN ARTHUR'S HAND HELD ALL THE EVIL IN THE WORLD. He could almost feel darkness and death swirling off it.

Walking from the train station to the Johnson Boarding House took far less time than he had wanted it to. Once he finished this, once he delivered what he had been given, he would have nothing left. No one. Nowhere to go.

Maybe that was best. He was tired down to his bones, exhausted and weary like a seventeen-year-old wearing an old man's body.

Arthur had scarcely dropped his hand from knocking when the door was flung open and he was greeted by a woman, everything about her soft and curled and warm. Her cheerful expression died in the breath of time it took for Mrs. Johnson to realize exactly who it was he reminded her of. She let out a whoosh of breath, collapsing beneath it, suddenly diminished.

"You must be Arthur." Her eyes searched his face as though she could make him look like someone else. Anyone else.

He couldn't blame her.

His own smile felt like a guilty lie on his face, tight and itchy as a sunburn. "I am. I have a letter for you." He dropped his case and pulled the resealed letter out of his suit jacket pocket.

A letter for Mrs. Johnson, he thought. *Accursed items for Mr. Johnson. Nothing for me.*

Mrs. Johnson took it, her palm sinking beneath the weight of unread words. "She's dead, isn't she?"

Arthur wanted to go inside. He felt exposed, standing alone on the porch. Maybe she wouldn't let him in. He wouldn't blame her. Maybe if she let him in, he'd immediately slip out the back and keep going, keep traveling, keep hiding.

He thought of his mother. Her pale, cold toes.

"Yes, she died last week."

He was unprepared for Mrs. Johnson to wrap her arms around him, trapping his arms at his sides and pulling him close. She smelled like flour and brown sugar.

What mothers are supposed to smell like.

His had always smelled of smoke and fear. The latter was her gift to him, his only inheritance. Her fear had chased her to the end of a rope. Arthur kept his fear at an angle, tucked it around himself. It was his friend, his constant companion.

Mrs. Johnson's white cotton cap rested against his chin and he didn't know what to do, how to move, how to accept this. He'd been uncomfortable in his body ever since he'd begun to outgrow the adults around him. Being a small boy had been easier. Quicker. There'd been more places to slip through, more places to hide. His mother had chided him for growing straight and tall, so he'd cultivated a talent for making other people's eyes slide past him. But how could he be unnoticed while being embraced?

Sniffling, Mrs. Johnson pulled back, keeping her hands on his arms and looking up into his eyes. Her face rearranged itself into a determined warmth. "Well, then. Come in. I'll make something for you to eat while I read this, and then we'll get you settled."

"Where is Mr. Johnson?" Arthur asked, nervously pulling on his tie, trying to tuck it into his vest, though both were too small. He wanted to leave. This town was beautiful, homes and a main street idyllically curled around the bay like a sleeping cat. But Arthur knew better. This was one of the bad places. One of the worst. His mother's voice whispered frantically in the back of his head, telling him to run, run, run.

Mrs. Johnson's expression deepened in its determination, more an act of will than anything else. "Mr. Johnson's been dead going on a year now. Come in, dear."

Arthur's shoulders collapsed. The case at his feet had no home. There was no one to pass it along to, no one left to inherit the curse of knowledge that had orphaned him. He drifted inside, pulled in the flour-wake of Mrs. Johnson's path. He was not free of it, then. And, even worse, now he had no path, nothing to keep him going, no goal.

Everything hurt much, much more.

"Make yourself comfortable, dear. I won't be a few minutes." Mrs. Johnson's assured steps into the kitchen were a well-masked retreat, and he wondered at how careful she was to hide what she was really feeling. Was she trying to *protect* him?

Hopeless.

The room he was in had two sofas, light blue with lace doilies on the arms, and a table between them. He didn't want to sit. His hand hovered over the case. He'd leave.

". . . will not make excuses for you again! If you don't do your own chores, so help me, I'll —"

Two teen girls, nearly mirror images of each other, stumbled to a shocked stop after entering the room. Both gaped at him.

The taller of the two wore her dress with an apron pinned precisely in front. Her face was round, her dark eyes solemn and piercing over a button nose and full lips. Everything about her was neat and marble, save a single curl that had escaped her cotton cap.

The shorter girl took nearly the same features and managed to look wild and fey. Her cheeks were pink and flushed, her eyes bright with mischief, her blouse untucked from her skirt. One stocking bunched around the top of her scuffed black shoe. Her hair, however, was perfectly pinned back beneath a blue ribbon.

"Who are you?" the shorter girl asked, chin tipped up and eyes narrowed in consideration. Arthur felt as though he were being read like a book, and wondered whether this girl would like his story. It was not a story *he* particularly liked.

"Minnie!" the other girl hissed, before turning back to him. "Hello. I'm Miss Johnson, and this is my sister."

The door to the kitchen banged open, held by Mrs. Johnson's hip as she balanced a tray. Without being asked, the taller girl rushed forward, taking the tea service. Minnie stayed where she was, her eyes never leaving their increasingly delighted study of Arthur.

"These are my daughters," Mrs. Johnson said, setting a plate of rolls and gravy on the low table in the middle of the room. "Cora, my eldest, and Minnie."

Cora smiled sweetly. Minnie went cross-eyed, then looked smugly at Cora to see her reaction.

"Girls, this is Arthur. He's family, and will be staying with us now."

Arthur didn't know who was more shocked, the girls or himself. "I —" he started, but Mrs. Johnson shot him a look that brooked no argument. He couldn't correct her, not now. He'd slip out tonight, into the darkness and shadows.

"Cora will show you the attic room when you've finished eating. We're very glad you're here. It will be nice to have a man in the house again." A tremor in her voice was the only indication that anything was wrong. That, and the way she looked just to the side of Arthur's face as she spoke, never making full eye contact.

Wiping her hands on her apron, she nodded and went back into the kitchen.

Minnie clapped her hands in delight. "Are you a cousin? I've always wanted a handsome cousin!"

Arthur shook his head, noticing a framed photograph hanging on the wall. "I don't think I am."

"A cousin, or handsome? Because you are certainly handsome, even if you aren't a cousin." Minnie's impish expression was knocked away by Cora's elbow digging into her ribs.

Wanting to escape Minnie's energetic attention, Arthur walked forward, looking at the sepia-captured face of the man who was supposed to inherit his secrets. Out of his reach forever. "I am sorry about your father's death."

"Did you know him?" Cora asked quietly.

"Yes." Arthur's voice matched her whisper. Mr. Johnson had been the one constant of his childhood. Wherever they were, he found them, brought food and money. He'd been the only thing that ever felt safe, the only man his mother trusted after his father disappeared.

Cora and Minnie shared a look heavy with questions and the conclusions they were jumping to. Primly clearing her throat, Cora asked, "How old are you?"

"Seventeen."

"So you were born before our parents got married," Minnie said, raising her eyebrows pointedly at Cora, as though demanding Cora ask the question they both wanted answered.

Arthur opened his mouth to correct them, but the truth felt too twisted. A part of him was deeply hurt by Mr. Johnson's absence when Arthur needed him most.

Let the girls think poorly of their father. I'm not staying, anyway.

Sensing that no explanation would be forthcoming, Cora leaned forward to grab the case. "I'll take your things up to your room, then," she said.

"No!" Arthur shouted, startling her so much that she dropped the bag. "I'm sorry. It's heavy, is all," he added, gentle guilt filling him. "You don't have to do anything for me."

"I don't mind," she assured him, with a genuine friendliness that he was deeply unused to.

For a moment Arthur hated them, hated that they had never known evil, had never had to hide.

But they've known loss, he reminded himself.

Mr. Johnson had left him, but he'd left his family, too. Alone and unprotected in this deadly town.

He watched as Cora carefully picked up his case. Minnie looked on, so innocent despite her attempt to look mischievous.

They have no idea.

And they have no one to protect them.

These words came to him in his own voice . . . but he could hear Mr. Johnson's safe haven of a voice underneath.

Protect them.

But that would mean staying.

For as long as it took.

That night, as the house lay sleeping, he slipped outside and into the trees surrounding the cheerful yellow boardinghouse, color leeched to a pale glow in the moonlight. Under the cover of darkness, he dug a hole deep enough for a body, then dropped his case inside.

He spit on it, wishing he could burn it, wishing he didn't fear what it held so much. He had promised his mother he would never look inside, but it was all he had left of his own father.

Into the ground with it, then — the same place the cursed items had put all those whose lives they'd tainted.

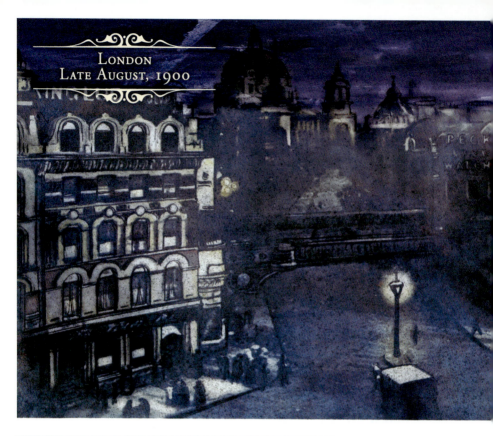

LONDON
LATE AUGUST, 1900

THREE

THOM'S FINGERS WERE RESTLESS, POUNDING THE NOTES VIOLENTLY INSTEAD OF THEIR USUAL CARESSING. At the end of the piece he slammed his fist into the keys, immediately regretting it as the grand piano's discordant burst sounded like pain.

He let his forehead drop onto the cool ivory, wishing music were the refuge it used to be. He couldn't fall deeply into it, couldn't immerse himself far enough to forget to worry.

Standing, he closed the lid carefully. He'd go out. Maybe someone else's music could pull him away from reality.

He buttoned a jacket over his vest and raked his fingers through his hair, slicking it into shape as he looked out over the New York City night. It glowed and twinkled back with the promise of escape.

Padding down the thickly carpeted hall, he turned the doorknob and eased open Charles's door. His younger brother lay diagonally across the bed, feet twisted in the sheets, comforter on the floor, his arm thrown over his face. He never used to sleep this way, but Thom had been finding him in this position more and more often. Charles claimed the pressure helped ease the headaches.

Thom tiptoed into the room, easing the comforter back over Charles's much-thinned frame. Charles's eyes twitched beneath his lids, rapidly processing dreams. Thom hoped they were dreams of running, dreams of light and life that would bring his brilliant brother back from the deathly chasms he walked now.

When Thom went out the front door minutes later, no one stopped him. No one ever did. At the dance hall, no one stopped him as he ran himself ragged, the syncopated rhythms of the ragtime beating out any other thoughts. He kissed a pretty girl who picked his pocket. He let her. He laughed and danced and did everything to excess and almost — almost — managed to forget.

When he stumbled home that night, he had just enough wits about him to do so quietly, tipping the elevator attendant extra as they reached the penthouse floor. Thom planned to slink down the hall toward his room but froze when he saw lights on in his father's office, leaking out beneath the door. What was his father doing home? He was never home. The last Thom had heard, his father was in Germany. Before that, London. Before that, Chicago.

Anywhere but here, anywhere but where his favorite son lay ill and his other son frantically tried to make it better, or numbly tried to escape when it wasn't. Edward Wolcott was a man who fixed problems. When the doctors had made it clear that Charles would never be fixed, well, he'd moved on to things that could.

Muffled voices drifted toward Thom, and he walked to the office door, leaning his head against the frame. At first Thom was confused, sluggishly failing to process what he was hearing. One of the men sounded like his father, but not the father he knew. Gone was the cold, imperious authority. Gone was the razor-sharp efficiency. His father sounded . . . scared. Pleading.

". . . surely something else can be arranged. There are all sorts of boys for the taking, anywhere you look in this city."

"The nature of a sacrificial offering is that sacrifice is required."

This other voice was calm, detached but pleasant. A woman. Thom scowled. Why was his father bringing a woman here? If they woke up Charles . . .

"You can't ask me to do this."

Thom let out a relieved breath. Here was the domineering man he knew. Even though they'd never gotten along, Thom realized he depended on the stability of his father's power.

Heeled footsteps echoed off the marble floor of the office, slow and uneven, as though the woman were walking around the room, examining it. "Willingly give one, or be stripped of all. Your decision. You agreed."

When Thom's father spoke again, he sounded as broken as Thom had felt since Charles had gotten sick. "I'll make the arrangements."

"There's a good boy," the woman said.

Thom barely made it around the corner before the office door opened. Unsettled and unable to ask his father what the conversation had been about, Thomas dragged his own pillow into Charles's room and slept on the floor, counting Charles's breaths until he finally fell into sleep.

The next morning Thom awoke with a pounding headache to find Charles leaning over the bed, grinning slyly at him.

"Had yourself a bit of a bash last night, I see."

Thom groaned, swatting ineffectively at his brother. But secretly he was thrilled, feeling lighter in spite of the pain. With Charles awake and teasing, it was going to be a good day. A hopeful day. "I heard some new ragtime," he croaked. "I think I remember enough to play it for you."

"Boys," their father interrupted from the doorway.

Charles raised an eyebrow quizzically, and Thom rubbed at his own forehead, renewed unease washing over him. If his father was here, that meant that last night hadn't been a dream.

"Come eat breakfast with me." It wasn't a request; it was a

command. Thom waited for Charles to ease out of bed and walked to the dining room with him.

They'd barely begun eating when their father leaned away from his untouched food and clicked his heavy gold pocket watch open and shut in a beatless tick that made Thom want to scream.

Finally their father snapped the watch shut and put it away. He didn't look at either of his sons as he said, "You're going away for the summer. To Maine, to take the ocean air for Charles's health. Agnes will pack your things."

Thom stuttered in disbelief, "Why? Since when?"

Their father stood, straightening his tie with a slight tremble in his fingers that Thom hadn't noticed before. "It's already decided."

He left the room without another word. Charles shrugged impassively at Thom. "Could be fun, right? Gotta smell better than the city in the summer."

Without answering, Thom hurried after their father, catching him at the elevator. "Dad?"

Edward Wolcott didn't turn around. The ramrod-straight lines of his shoulders and back were sloped today. Everything was off, everything was wrong.

"Why are we going to Maine? And who was that woman here last night?"

When Thom's father turned to face him, his steel-gray eyes looked haunted. "Your brother is dying," he whispered.

Though Thom knew it was true — had known for months now — hearing it spoken like an inevitability shook him to his core.

"He's not," Thom said, stubbornly willing it to be true, hating his father for saying death out loud and making it even more real.

The elevator opened and Thom turned away angrily. As he stomped back to the door, his father whispered, "Please forgive me."

It was the first time Thom had ever heard his father use the word *please*.

It terrified him.

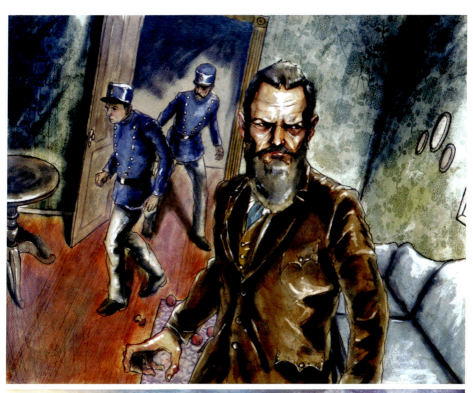

FOUR

CHARLES HAD DISCOVERED, MUCH TO HIS SURPRISE, THAT DYING CAME WITH A WHOLE ARRAY OF BENEFITS.

Certainly there was much to be said for *not* dying before the age of sixteen, but as that did not appear to be an option, he had reconciled himself to slamming into the end of his life with as much momentum as he could manage.

He knew Thom was angry to be torn away from the city he loved, but the Johnson Boarding House seemed nice enough. One place was much the same as any other as far as Charles was concerned. He could tell from the way Thom twitched next to him at the table, fingers tapping Beethoven on his legs, that they would have to devise an escape from these group dinners, though.

Beethoven meant Thom was angry. Charles needed to switch him onto Mozart. Or, better yet, ragtime. A lively ragtime summer was preferable to a glowering Beethoven one.

A woman who had introduced herself as Mrs. Humphrey sat at the head of the table, scooping copious amounts of sugar into her tea while darting glances around to see if anyone noticed. A fine dusting of the sweet crystals clung to her vast bosom, which, owing to her short and round stature, rested on the table in front of her.

She had cooed at him, tsking softly at his pallid complexion. Illness made people either avoid him or pamper him, and she was in the latter category. It could come in handy, now that he'd lost his most malleable nurses.

A honeymooning couple, who fell firmly in the avoid-acknowledging-the-sick-boy category, were remarking on the quality of the day and planning a bicycle ride to the lighthouse.

There was another young man probably around Thom's age. He clung to the edges, slipping in after introductions, face neither angry nor pleasant. Everything about him begged to be ignored in the most polite sort of way. He looked to be no fun at all.

There was also a man with a full mustache. He was tall, shoulders several inches above the curved wooden back of his chair, filling out the lines of his finely tailored suit. Something in the line of his mouth spoke of age to Charles, the gradual, wearing weight of time. Forty? No, the man's skin was free of wrinkles and his hair was a slick, glossy brown, save a streak of gray. Was there a polite way of asking what his age was? It would bother Charles, not knowing. He liked to categorize things, filter and sort and understand and —

A girl of sixteen or seventeen swept into the room, picture-pretty and efficiently elegant, and Charles no longer cared a whit about the man. He leaned back, letting a smile play over his mouth in anticipation. Girls were problems to be solved, and he was *very* good at solving problems.

"Thank you, Cora," Mrs. Humphrey said. *Cora!* He liked the shape of the name, the motion of the lips it required.

The silent young man sat straight in his chair. Until that movement Charles had forgotten he was there. The boy was glaring in alarm at something, so Charles followed his gaze.

The mustachioed man's eyes followed Cora's movement and a slow, creeping leer spread across his face until his upper lip disappeared beneath his mustache. Charles fought the urge to mimic the other boy's posture of alarm. Cora continued, oblivious. When she passed the man, Charles saw him breathe in deeply, as though inhaling her.

Mrs. Johnson, wearing the same white apron as Cora over a body thickened by age and childbirth, followed her daughter with a pitcher of lemonade garnished with fresh mint. She paused in front of the young man, who shook his head slowly, then looked deliberately at the man, then Cora, then back to Mrs. Johnson.

In the sudden firming of her jaw and tightening of her lips, Charles knew the threat had been communicated. She nodded and the boy let his eyes drift to the corner where the wall met the ceiling.

Interesting. Charles settled back to watch how it would play out. He liked learning how things worked — automobiles, factories, people. People were not so very different from machines. Once you figured out how all of the parts interacted, you could very nearly tell what would happen before it occurred. It was clear the mysterious boy was part of the machinery of this household, and thus worth noting.

After supper, Charles engaged Thom in a silly argument over something in the paper as an excuse to linger after all the guests besides the young man left. When Cora came in to clear dishes, Mrs. Johnson followed.

"Cora," she said, "you work too hard. You ought to have a free summer, like you did when you were a little girl."

"I'm not Minnie," Cora said with a frown, continuing to stack plates. "You need me."

"Minnie?" Charles asked, flashing a dimple to atone for interrupting.

"My other daughter," Mrs. Johnson said. "She ought to have been down, but . . ."

"But she's dotty," Cora muttered.

Mrs. Johnson turned back to Cora. "I think you should spend as much time as possible outside in the fresh air. Come fall, you'll finish your schooling and never have a summer like this again. I've been meaning to bring the O'Connell girl on, and she'll be more than enough help for me and Minnie."

"I can't simply do *nothing* this summer."

Charles watched the studied, careful nonchalance of Mrs. Johnson's delivery, and the way the other boy listened intently while pretending to do nothing at all. Ah! They were trying to keep Cora out of the house, and away from the attentions of that man. Which told Charles that they needed the boarder's money, but that Mrs. Johnson was well aware of her daughter's safety, and partnered with the boy to secure it.

"Actually," Charles said, adding a bit of extra wheeze to his voice, "if I could be so bold, my father had talked of hiring a companion, but companions are always stuffy old women who smell like cats. I loathe cats. Couldn't we pay extra to have Cora and Minnie look after us this summer?"

Thom sputtered in embarrassment next to him, and Charles stomped hard on his foot under the table. If Minnie were half as pretty as her sister, he might have stumbled on a way to keep Thom happy this summer, too.

Charles continued earnestly. "I think some fun companions would be just the thing for me." He coughed, looking up at Cora and Mrs. Johnson with eyes large and winsome. The mystery boy met Charles's gaze suspiciously. Charles was making himself part of the machinery now.

"It's settled, then." Mrs. Johnson patted Cora's shoulder as Cora stood still, arms full of dishes, mouth open in shock. "And Arthur, of course, will keep an eye on you and Minnie for me."

The other boy, Arthur, had effectively been assigned to be a chaperone. That'd make things trickier, depending on his relation to the girls. But Charles was very confident in his summer prospects now, and had the added pride of having helped nice Mrs. Johnson keep her daughter safe. Everybody won.

After she took the dishes from Cora, Mrs. Johnson called over her shoulder, "And all of you please remember to keep your bedroom doors locked at night after you turn in for bed. House rule."

"Brilliant!" Charles said, standing and holding out a hand for Cora to shake. "Thanks so much."

"Oh, of course. I — it'll be fun." Cora's voice trailed off. She sounded a bit lost. Charles would make sure she didn't stay lost. She needed a task.

"Is there somewhere outside to sit?" he asked. "The evening looks nice."

"Yes! Of course. The veranda. Would you like a blanket? I can make a tea service! But first, come this way." She walked purposefully out of the room.

"What're you on about?" Thom growled behind Charles as they followed Cora through the main floor of the house and out the back door to a veranda completely boxed in by an ivy-covered trellis.

Charles whispered over his shoulder, "Oh, I'm sorry, did you want to spend the whole summer watching me struggle for breath? Because I think Cora is much prettier to look at than I am." Charles sat on a cushioned bench, pleased with himself. Things were shaping up nicely.

A girl's voice above them let out a muffled curse, followed by a thump overhead that made them all jump. Charles looked up but couldn't see anything through the leafy green filter of the ivy.

"Minnie Johnson, you get down here right this instant," Cora hissed, hands on her hips.

The trellis roof above them shook, and then a face hung upside down from atop the arched exit to the garden. "Boys!" Minnie gasped, her upside-down smile brighter than the veranda lamps casting golden highlights on her dark curls. Her head disappeared. The trellis shook again, like the girl was crawling across the top of it. Then there was a falling sound and a scream. Thom stood and rushed toward the veranda's exit, but the scream was cut short by a laugh.

Arthur melted free of the shadows, Minnie caught in his arms. Charles had forgotten about him, hadn't even noticed him follow them out. Or had he gone a different way? Arthur set Minnie down on the ground, then leaned against the arch just out of reach of the lamplight.

"Aren't you going to introduce us?" Minnie asked, and Charles was delighted to note that Thom was no longer playing Beethoven. Even his fingers had been stunned into silence when presented with not one but two beautiful girls, both of whom belonged to them this summer thanks to Charles.

Charles was an excellent brother when he set his mind to it.

Cora spoke first. "This is Charles, and this is Thomas. They're boarding here for the summer, which you would know if you'd helped with supper service like you were supposed to."

Minnie's mouth set in an embarrassed frown as she deliberately lifted her eyebrows, not looking at the strange new boys Cora had just scolded her in front of. "Shouldn't you be cleaning?" she asked her sister. "Surely there's some lonely corner left to sweep."

Cora folded her arms crossly. "No. We're . . . I'm not . . . our *job* this summer is to keep Thomas and Charles company." Before Minnie could utter whatever delightful thing was about to leave her mouth, Cora snapped, "Where are your shoes?"

"Put very carefully away so you can't scold me for leaving them out. Now," she said, clapping her hands together, eyes dancing, "who is ready for an adventure?"

Thom leaned back with a sigh. "What with the travel and all, we ought to —"

"Go on the most daring adventure you can think of," Charles interrupted. "Otherwise we'll miss New York too much. What do you have that New York doesn't?"

A worried crease between her brows, Cora bit her lip thoughtfully. "There are the caves at the beach —"

"As old as time, and haunted!" Minnie declared.

Cora scowled but continued as though she hadn't been interrupted. "— which are a very short walk. We can visit the lighthouse tomorrow, if you'd like, and the church is —"

"No one cares about the church!" Minnie cried, a pleased and sly cast to her eyes as she watched Cora's reaction to her reaction. "They can see a church anywhere." She turned to the brothers. "Let me ask you this: How many *witches* did you have in New York City?"

Charles matched Minnie's grin, noting Cora's dismay but too caught up in the magnetism of Minnie's dark, glittering eyes to care. If Cora was an engine keeping everything running, Minnie was both steering wheel and gas pedal. He was very curious to see where she'd drive them.

"I have yet to meet a single witch in our great metropolis," he said.

"Then we have you beat." Minnie skipped off the steps and into the night, beckoning them to follow with her mocking laugh. "Come on, come on!"

To the witch! Charles thought, giddy with the thrill of doing something besides dying. Arthur held out his arm to Cora, who took it, casting a worried glance back toward the house.

As he and Thom stepped into the night, Charles felt an odd weight on the back of his neck and looked up. In one of the second-story windows, a figure stood, silhouetted in black, impossible to identify. Watching them.

Charles rubbed his shoulder against his ear, trying to shake off a sudden chill. But it wouldn't leave.

FIVE

MINNIE SPUN AND TWIRLED, THE DIRT ROAD STILL WARM UNDERFOOT. It wasn't the height of tourist season yet, and the town still felt like it belonged only to her at night.

She knew it like no one else did. She divined all its secrets, and gave it even more. It was a land woven together by stories, threaded through with magic. Lately no one saw the magic but her, and it broke her heart.

But tonight! Tonight she had two new boys, and her Arthur. She'd even managed to get Cora out.

In Minnie's darkest moods, which struck like storms from the sea, brutal and overpowering and then gone without a trace, she hated her father for dying. Her father's death had killed the sister she knew, and replaced fun, dazzling, brave Cora with a soft and prim version of their mother.

Minnie *had* a mother. She wanted her Cora again.

A small worm of guilt wriggled through her stomach. She knew it wasn't right to force Cora to come along with them to spy on the witch. Minnie knew how terrified Cora had been that day, knew that she still woke with nightmares.

But curse that witch, Minnie hated who her sister had become. Maybe another trip would finally convince her that their father's heart attack had nothing to do with Cora climbing that wretched tree.

Maybe, as Minnie sometimes suspected, the witch had stolen part of her sister's soul through the small cut at the back of Cora's head.

In which case Minnie would simply have to steal it back.

"Are you twins?" one of the brothers asked. Thomas. He was taller, but Charles was handsomer, with a sort of tragic romance to his face, and Minnie fancied him immediately for it. She fancied nearly everyone, though, and never let it bother her to distraction. There was only one person her heart held close, but it was a secret, and a dangerous one to nourish.

She glanced at Cora on Arthur's arm and burned with jealousy.

Best to focus on the boys she could be certain she was not related to. It would hurt far less.

"We're eleven months apart," Cora answered.

"Irish twins, then. And Arthur is your . . . ?" Charles said, letting the sentence end to form a question.

"Our mysterious relative," Minnie cut in joyfully, glad to have an excuse to talk about him and try to get a reaction. Maybe, for once, Arthur would actually answer.

"Bite your tongue!" Cora gasped. "He is *not* related to us! He is a friend of the family."

"Oh, they'd hear the speculation eventually. Is it any kinder to whisper it behind his back? Arthur doesn't mind, do you?"

"I am the least interesting mystery in town," he offered.

Minnie waved dismissively, disappointed as always by Arthur's deflection. Weaving her hand through Charles's elbow, she continued. "Arthur has been with us a year now, and we're very tired of his mystery and ever so glad to have some boarders who aren't too old to have any adventures left. Why are you here?" She trained her big brown eyes on Charles, willing him to say something interesting. Gypsies or gangsters or sinister family secrets — she would take anything that would give her an excuse to romanticize him further. Though if he *were* actually dying, as she had overheard while hiding in the pantry this afternoon, that was romantic enough for her needs. Nearly as good as one of her Gothic novels!

Charles shrugged, grinning pleasantly. "We're here to take the air."

"And where, pray tell, are you going to take it?" Arthur murmured, giving a suspicious glare at Minnie's and Charles's linked arms. This filled Minnie with a spark of hope she tried to stifle.

"And how," she said, ignoring Arthur's glare by walking even closer to Charles, "does one transport air once it's been taken? I should think your luggage quite full of clothes."

Cora tugged on the lock that always fell down over her forehead. Sometimes Minnie found herself brushing her own forehead as though Cora were a distorted mirror. "Please pay them no mind," Cora said to Charles. "They can never end until one of them has said something so silly the other cannot beat it." She was all jangling nerves, spooking any time a bird called, watching the familiar lanes as if at any moment something would jump out at them. It gave Minnie both a triumphant thrill and a pang of conscience to see how scared she was.

Charles was not going to be left out of the fun, though. "Air is best transported in lungs, which is why I brought Thom with me. He's going to store the extra I can't fit. My father likes to get his money's worth."

"He certainly does . . . ," Thomas muttered. He was neither scared nor excited, and watched Charles like he feared his brother would drop dead at any moment. Minnie didn't care for Thomas. He was decidedly too much like the new Cora.

Cora's hand went to her apron pocket, worrying a stone worn smooth these last two years. The line between her brows deepened as she let go of Arthur's arm and looked back toward the boardinghouse, now out of view. "We were given specific instruction to be very careful of Charles's health."

Charles gallantly took her now-free hand and put it on his other arm. "That's easy, then. I've left my health upstairs in a trunk where it can't possibly come to any harm."

Arthur eyed the action as warily as he had with Minnie, which was a disappointment. He was always watching Cora, their mother, and Minnie. She sometimes caught him lurking about, prowling around the boardinghouse at night. She'd been secretly catching him at it since the day he arrived. Arthur was a mystery, her very own mystery, both the best and worst part of every day.

His eyes were like the ocean. Sometimes they were blue, sometimes they were green, and sometimes they were so dark they were no color at all. Minnie always tried to guess what color they would be at a given moment; she was almost never right.

He was forever trying not to be seen, but she saw him.

She wound a circular path, cutting through backyards and private property, tramping across the town as though she owned it, which, at night, she did. In the daylight, order ruled, fences stood, how-do-you-do's and polite nods were the recipe. But at night, darkness rendered everything still and hush and secret. Minnie was a curator of secrets.

Finally they came round a bend in the lane and their destination appeared. A two-storied house, steep-roofed and turreted, stood sentinel on top of a small hill. Around it, scarred through with the two dirt lines of the lane, the yard dropped into a sea of night-black trees. Much as she feared it, like all the other children who grew up here, she also loved the house, and sometimes daydreamed it was hers.

The group had never agreed what they were expecting to find once they got here, but it certainly wasn't this much light dripping from the windows on the first story.

"So, about this witch," Thomas said, fingers tapping on his leg. "What's the story there?"

"Why don't you tell them, Cora?" Minnie's voice dripped with syrup, all false sweetness.

"Shut up," Cora snapped. It was the most spirit Minnie had seen from her in ages, and only proved to Minnie that this whole excursion was a grand idea.

"She never leaves," Minnie whispered as they crept up the hill, Charles and Thomas next to her, Arthur drifting back with Cora. "She's lived here for as long as anyone can remember, though no one has ever actually spoken with her. No one . . . except Cora." She glanced over her shoulder to see Arthur whispering intently in Cora's ear, both of them yards behind now and out of hearing range. Minnie wanted to win over Thomas as much as she had Charles, even if he *was* stuffy. So she only felt mildly wicked as she fed them an exaggerated horror even she didn't believe. "The witch nearly killed my sister, and she sent her familiars out that night to steal the rest of Cora's soul. But familiars are blind, and when they got to our house, they took my father's soul instead."

Charles looked delighted by the tale, and Minnie scowled. It was not the reaction she had been hoping for. She opened her mouth to try something scarier, but another set of sounds interrupted the air. They all stopped, holding their breath to listen.

"Is that — that's ragtime!" Thomas said, stopping in amazement.

"'Maple Leaf Rag'! She must have a phonograph!" Charles said. "You thought no one would have one here. Apparently Minnie and Cora's reclusive witch has excellent taste in music."

As one, the three in the lead moved toward the nearest lit window, slinking low to the ground beneath the sill. Cora and Arthur followed.

"I get first peek," Minnie whispered.

"Guest rules." Charles grinned at her. "I should get first."

"I don't want to look at all. You may have my turns," Cora said, leaning her shoulder against the wood siding of the house and staring out into the night. Her breathing was even, but Minnie could see that she was trembling.

Thomas shrugged. "All at once. Just don't stick your head up any higher than you need to. Cora, keep your eyes peeled for familiar spirits or bats or whatever it is witches employ to guard against Peeping Charleses."

Minnie trembled, too, with either excitement or fear, which were so often indistinguishable until afterward when she knew the result of the event. Flanked by Arthur and Thomas, she raised her eyes past the sill to peer into the witch's home.

A woman, slender as a willow tree and wearing not much more than her slip, danced madly across the room, throwing her body to the beats of Joplin's ragtime, her floor-length braid whipping like a living thing. Her eyes were closed, and, though the room blazed with lamps, Minnie couldn't say exactly what color her hair was, or even what she looked like. The witch was all wild movement and snaking hair.

"What's going on?" Cora whispered.

"She's dancing. Have a look." Arthur shifted over to give Cora room, nearly knocking everyone else down. After some glares and hisses, there was just enough room for Cora to see, too.

"She dances like you," Charles said, punching Thomas lightly on the back.

Minnie hoped this was weird and funny enough that perhaps Cora would forget to be careful and frightened all the time now.

The song neared the end and, out of place with the rest of her mad choreography, the witch climbed up onto a ladder propped against the wall, balance precarious as she lifted her arms to the ceiling beams and laughed. Even through the glass, her cackle was a mad thing, twisted discordant notes, rising above the sound of the music. She shook violently, and Minnie realized she may have been sobbing. She felt suddenly shamed to be witness to this, and her eyes fixed on the witch's pale, slender feet, toes curled around a rung. Minnie's gaze followed the twining length up to where the witch's braid was wrapped around her neck.

Not her braid, she realized.

"No!" Minnie screamed as the woman jumped off the ladder and snapped at the end of the rope.

Congratulations on the twins, and give my best to lovely Lillian. I am still in pursuit of our enemies, however, I too am hunted. My deepest apologies for your burden as always. In return, the blue envelope is for you and your family. The other is to be added to the rest. Someday we will have enough to finally realize our end goal.

Thank you again for your help.

With gratitude

SIX

A HIGH, KEENING SCREAM, MORE ANIMAL THAN HUMAN, HUNG ON THE AIR. Until she had to gasp for breath, Cora did not know the sound was coming from her own mouth.

The break in her scream signaled the end of the horrified trance the five companions were under. Thomas let out a string of oaths, while Minnie and Charles collapsed into each other. Arthur simply stared.

"We've got to help her!" Cora stood, wanting to look away from the gently swinging body of the witch. The song was still going, bright syncopated rhythms jarring with the slow death dance.

Cora looked down, breaking her fingernails against the bottom of the window frame. There was a door, somewhere, but the window was their portal to this horror, and she had to get through it — she had to get through — she had to help, had to stop this from having happened.

It was her fault. The witch had warned Cora that death was at her heels, and now she had brought it here. She hadn't wanted this.

Had she?

"She's dead." Arthur's voice sounded as though it were coming from a very far distance. "If she were choking, she'd be twitching. Her neck is snapped."

"How do you know?" Thomas said, helping Cora with the window to no avail.

Arthur took Cora's hands and held them in his own, turning her away from the glass. He didn't look at Thomas as he answered. "I've seen a hanged body before."

"We need —" Cora took a deep breath. She could still see the woman's white slip behind her closed eyes. "We need to get Daniel. He lives closer than the police chief."

"She's already dead. We weren't supposed to be here. It won't do any good for anyone." Arthur's voice was a murmur blending into the night sounds. The music had stopped, leaving nothing but the breeze whispering secrets to the trees; Cora couldn't tell whether the quiet made things feel better or worse.

"I won't have her left like that." Cora pulled her hands away from Arthur, shoving one into her skirt pocket and running the other through her hair. "No one comes here. It could be a week or more before someone discovers her. She doesn't deserve that." Her voice broke and she closed her eyes, trying to take comfort from the worn stone in her pocket. She didn't want the witch dead. She didn't. This wasn't her fault.

There was work to be done, and she would do it. Work was her salvation. "Minnie," she said, "take Charles home."

Minnie and Charles still huddled on the ground, holding on to each other. Charles's breathing was fast, his eyes unnaturally bright. Minnie looked up at Cora, anguish written on her features. "I didn't know," she whispered. "I just wanted . . . I just wanted to have another story with you."

"Go *home*, Minnie! Now!"

Her sister's shoulders folded in on themselves, no trace of wild energy left. For a moment Cora leaned forward, wanting to take Minnie into her arms, to whisper sweet stories in her ear, to share warm, safe secrets in a space all their own.

But no. No stories. Minnie's stories had done enough for one night, and a wave of resentment washed away Cora's tender impulses.

Thomas helped Charles up. "Go slowly," he said. He frowned as he watched the two of them walk back down the hill, arms around each other as though both were on the verge of falling.

"You should go with them," Cora said. She brushed off the front of her skirts and set her jaw determinedly, betrayed only by the slightest trembling.

Thomas took off his jacket and put it around her; his shirt was striped, accentuating the long, lean lines of his arms and slope of his shoulders. Earlier today Cora had thought him quite handsome. Now they all looked like ghostly photographs of themselves — washed out and indistinct.

"I'm not leaving you to this business alone," Thomas said. "We all decided to come. I'll see it through." They set off down the hill and onto the lane together. Arthur followed, a silent constant.

"We were taking a walk for my brother's health," Thomas said as they neared a tiny cottage set off from the road, the trees around slowly reclaiming the yard for the forest. "You and Minnie and Arthur came along at our request so we wouldn't get lost on unfamiliar streets. We heard music playing loudly and wondered if something was wrong. Charles and Minnie turned around because he was tired, and the three of us went up the hill to check things out. When we got to the window we saw her, already hanging."

Cora looked down at her feet as they slid out from under her skirt and back again. The burden of this lie hung heavy on her shoulders already. "We should have stopped her," she whispered, a tightness in her chest threatening to overwhelm her.

"She would have done it whether or not we were there." Thomas sounded angry, and Cora flinched until she realized he was talking to himself more than anyone else. "It would have happened no matter what. We couldn't have stopped it." He paused, and looked suddenly so tired she wondered whether the weight on his shoulders wasn't more than just tonight. He shrugged as though trying to wriggle out from beneath something. "We didn't do anything wrong."

"Then why are we lying?" Cora wiped at her face. The world that she had worked so hard to make ordered and peaceful in the airless, aching absence of her father had shifted into one of Minnie's stories, and she didn't know how to put everything back into place. She knew — had always known — that house was nothing but death.

At least it isn't Minnie, Cora thought with a ferocity that startled her. *The witch can take the burden of death this time.*

She raised her fist and knocked on Daniel's door, the rough grains providing a stinging reproach against her knuckles. She waited a few moments and then knocked again.

A thump and a muffled curse came from inside, followed by a gravelly caution to wait. The seams of the door came to life with the glow of a lantern before it opened and Daniel stood, in a nightshirt with trousers pulled on beneath. His light hair was mussed, the remains of pomade causing the back to stick up in a way she would have smiled at another time.

"Cora?" he asked, squinting out at them. "Is your mother hurt? What's wrong?"

"No, not my mother. I'm sorry. I —" The words lodged in her throat. Daniel had only recently been promoted to deputy. Not four summers ago they had sat together with the other local children on the banks of the creek, watching their feet turn violent red and tingly from the chill of the water, laughing at Minnie's face deliberately smeared with wild berries to look like blood. That vision of light-drenched youth broke against the night around her, scattering away into pieces she'd never find again.

Growing up, she found, was a heartbreaking endeavor.

"Come inside, you look about to faint. Is that Arthur? And who's this?"

"Thomas Wolcott, sir. We've got some bad news."

Cora leaned against the door frame, barely hearing the story as Thomas laid it out. She felt heavy and thick with guilt. If she had stayed at home, if she had stayed in bed, it wouldn't have happened. She felt in her bones that seeing it had made it happen, that she had pulled death right to the witch's door.

"Oh, Mary." Daniel said the woman's name like a prayer, and Cora felt it pierce her heart and drop down to the ground.

Mary.

Daniel pulled on a coat, buttoning it slowly over his nightshirt. "Come on, then," he said, wearier than the hour alone could account for. When had he grown so old? Was the same weight of living traced into Cora's own face now?

"Sir, do you want us to go with you?" Thomas asked.

"It's too late and too far to go for the chief. I'll need help getting her body down. Not right to leave her until morning."

"I'll take Cora home," Arthur said, and Cora saw the way the other two men startled, looking to the corner of the bottom step where Arthur was. Cora never forgot he was near, but everyone else seemed to. Except Minnie, who always dragged him out of the shadows.

"No, I want to come. She needs —" She squeezed her eyes shut against the vision of the witch — Mary — swaying at the end of her life. "She needs something over her slip before any more people see her. I should do that."

The walk back to the hill took far less time than it ought to have. Before Cora could steel herself for the task ahead, they were bathed in the falsely warm light of the window. Arthur let out a sharp hiss of a breath. Cora snapped her eyes up and looked through the window.

There was no one there.

"Where is she?" Thomas cried, pressing his hands to the glass. There was no body, no rope. The ladder stood against the wall, apparently innocent of its role as accomplice.

Daniel's voice had a wary edge to it now. "You said she hanged herself in this room?"

"She did! We saw it! She was right there!" Thomas jabbed his finger against the glass. "Someone must have moved the body."

Without another word, Daniel strode past them. Cora didn't know whether to follow or stay put; either way, her feet wouldn't move. She and Thomas and Arthur had taken twenty minutes at most to return. Mary wasn't just gone — the entire scene had been cleared, rewritten.

"The doors are all locked," Daniel said when he returned. "I knocked and there was no answer. You're certain you saw what you thought you saw?"

"We did! We all did." Thomas remained at his post by the window, staring in as though if he looked away things might re-arrange themselves again. "Someone must have come."

"There's no one in there. Cora, I —" Daniel shook his head, looking away. "We all expect this kind of thing from Minnie, but not from you. Leave Mary alone."

She shook her head in tiny, fluttering movements. "No, no, I would never . . . I'm sorry, we thought . . . we saw . . ." She bowed her head, defeated by the mysteries of the night. "I'm sorry."

"Go home," Daniel growled, shrugging his coat closer. "And keep better company, Cora, or I'll have words with your mother." He strode down the hill and away from them.

"I know what I saw," Thomas said, finally tearing his eyes away from the window to fix them on Cora and Arthur with an angry intensity. "You saw it, too. We all saw it."

Cora stared at the room with a dull, creeping dread, the scar on her scalp tight beneath her hair. If death hadn't claimed Mary, that meant it was still lurking, looking for someone else to take.

"We were wrong," she whispered. "We need to leave."

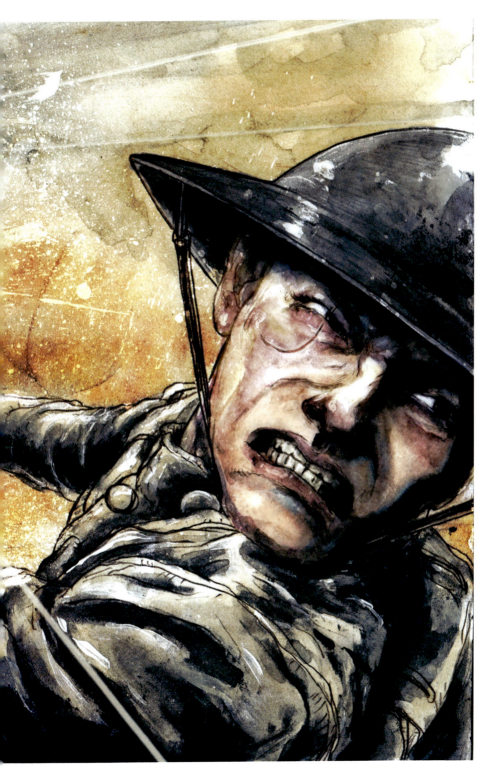

SEVEN

ARTHUR WAS WELL AWARE OF WHAT HAPPENED WHEN SOMEONE DROPPED TO THE END OF A ROPE AND DID NOT TWITCH. There was no slow suffocating death, no choking out of life. No chance to save her.

He hadn't been meant to be home when it had happened, but back then he'd rarely been where he was supposed to be. If his mother had known he was there, she wouldn't have done it. She would have done it eventually, but not then, not when he would see and try and fail to save her. She'd loved him very much, and he knew it.

But it hadn't stopped her from leaving him.

Arthur knew that the woman who'd hanged herself inside this house tonight was not his mother. He knew she had nothing to do with him, but she was important to Cora in some strange way, and so she was important to him, too. He needed to understand what had happened so he could take the memory of the snap at the end of a rope and place it into a box and bury that box with all the other boxes buried in the dark corners of his mind.

He watched, silent and unmoving, as Thomas paced angrily.

"We were not wrong! We did not all *imagine* the same thing! I don't know if it was a trick, or . . ." Thomas paused, mouth narrowing to a dark slash across his face. "If you planned this, if you all got together and thought you'd scare us, I swear I'll —"

"Shut up," Arthur said, his voice low. "We all saw it." He reached into his vest pocket and pulled out his lock pick, then walked toward the front of the house.

"Where are you going?" Cora asked.

"Inside."

By the time Cora and Thomas caught up to him, Arthur was already crouched in front of the door, working the lock. Though they could not see it, he was angry, too, his swift, sure fingers shaking as they worked the lock. He could taste his rage; it was hard and metallic and no amount of swallowing rid him of it.

When the lock slid out of place with the familiar soft snicking sound, he had no choice but to go into the house.

"We can't go in there!" Thomas said from behind him, but Arthur walked directly forward, not even sidling along the edge of the wall or looking for other ways to leave the room. He glanced back only once to see he was followed by Thomas, whose presence felt like the itchy tightness of salt water drying on skin. Cora did not follow. That was better.

They were not likely to be alone in the house, and if it were a *good* person who had taken Mary's body down, he would have answered the door when Daniel had knocked. This did not worry Arthur. He trusted wicked people far more than good people, because wicked people acted in their own best interest, whereas good people's actions often made no sense at all.

The room, lit to wanton brightness by candles and lamps scattered about on various tables and even the floor, was cluttered with mismatched furniture. Arthur traced his fingers along a writing desk; there was no note, nothing freshly written. A packet of letters, unopened, addressed to a Mary Smith. Something about the writing tickled the back of his mind, and he tucked them into his vest, along with a sharp letter opener.

"What are we doing in here?" Thomas asked, standing in the middle of the room, eyes darting about as though hanging were contagious.

Arthur walked past a low green sofa to where the simple wood ladder leaned against the wall. He looked to the exposed beam rafters of the ceiling, but there was no trace of the rope. The phonograph sat on a table near the chair, the round black record still in place.

There was a dim hallway leading toward the back of the house and the stairs, but Arthur felt Cora's presence outside like a magnet. He'd already had to lose track of Minnie for the night, and he refused to be farther from both of them than absolutely necessary. He didn't know Mary, but he did not trust odd happenings. Not in this town.

Other than the hallway, there was a door in the wall immediately opposite of where they had watched through the window. He crossed to it and the door slid open easily; the room on the other side was dark.

"Here," Thomas whispered behind him, holding a candle. Arthur nodded, surprised the other boy was paying enough attention to be helpful. The candle's flame threw everything into a riddle of deep shadows and orange echoes. The room appeared to be made entirely of books. All the walls, floor to ceiling, were lined with spines and shelves. Other than a sofa, the room was devoid of anything else. Arthur wanted to look at the books, but there were too many.

His father had always been surrounded by books, too. They painted a picture of a man obsessed with strange alternate histories, conspiracies, dark secrets. Paranoia that got him laughed out of his professorship. Mary's books would doubtless tell stories about who she was as well.

"Nothing," Arthur said, starting to turn, when someone in the shadows of the room moved.

"Look out!" Thomas cried, and they both jumped back before realizing they were seeing a reflection of themselves.

Trying to calm his racing heart, Arthur stepped forward and stared into the mirror.

"Come see this," he whispered. Thomas stood next to him and his brow furrowed. Another mirror was placed on the wall directly opposite so the two reflected each other. Now that they stood between them, it created an eternity of Thomas and Arthur in a dark flickering tunnel. The candle leeched the color from their faces so their features were all contrast — pale cheekbones and lips, dark holes for eyes. After the second image repetition, the details were hazy enough that the boys could have been each other or no one at all.

"Looks a bit like my vision of hell," Thomas whispered.

"At least there's good company." Arthur's reflection gave a ghost of a smile, and Thomas's met it.

"What's that?" Thomas leaned forward, touching a pendant hanging from the top of the mirror. "A bug?"

Arthur grabbed Thomas's hand, surprising the other boy into dropping the candle, which sputtered out. The walls of books leaned in, leering, and the old familiar breathless terror Arthur hadn't felt since his mother had died now twitched through his muscles, begging him to run, run, *run* into the night, find a new town, find a new life, find a new place to hide.

He had seen a necklace like that before. The green beetle figure at the end of the chain was featured in every portrait his father collected, was scribbled in the endless, illegible notes Arthur had flipped through as a child, was even engraved on an ancient book his mother had used to prop up their kitchen table.

His father had been clutching a necklace just like it the last time they'd ever seen him.

Seeing the necklace here ended all his nights trying to tell himself that his father had been crazy, had poisoned his mother's mind, had merely abandoned them instead of meeting a horrible fate. The green beetle meant that whatever dark secrets his father had chased and been consumed by . . .

They were real.

"Arthur!" Thomas hissed.

"This is a bad place," Arthur said. The initial shock of dread had settled into its old home in his bones now. The necklace wasn't meant for him. He was never meant to see it. Unlike his father, he wouldn't chase any of this. If they got out now, without being caught, then maybe he wouldn't have to run.

A soft creaking, the step of a light foot on the floor above them, had the same effect as a gunshot. Thomas and Arthur ran from the room just as they heard Cora scream outside.

Thomas was through the door first and down the porch steps in a single leap. Arthur thought he'd keep going, but without pausing, Thomas scooped Cora up from where she had fainted to the ground, throwing her over his shoulder and continuing his mad race into the night.

Arthur flew like their shadow down the hill, silent companion to Thomas's crashing footfalls. When they reached the bottom, Thomas kept going, never looking back.

Arthur wanted to do the same, more than anything. He wanted to fly and keep flying, to melt into the trees and disappear. He wanted to never have seen that beetle, the one his mother, weeping, sometimes drew on the skin over his heart, whispering about protection. He stopped instead, and turned back toward the house.

There, on the second floor, a silhouette marked their retreat. As he watched, a dark hand raised and pressed itself against the glass.

They had been seen.

NEW ORLEANS
MARDI GRAS PARADE &
AFTERMATH
MARCH 4, 1924

EIGHT

FOUR DAYS LATER, THOM HAD YET TO FIGURE OUT WHAT HE HAD SEEN THAT NIGHT. The excitement had taken a toll on Charles's fragile health, and Thom had stayed indoors to take care of him, despite the ministrations of all the women about. Arthur remained elusive, and Cora never wanted to talk — since she had woken up in his arms on that long walk home, she couldn't so much as look at him without blushing. He had to admit he felt oddly exposed, too. For all the girls he'd danced with and kissed in dark corners, there was something intimate about being there the moment Cora had awakened after so much fright.

Minnie was no help with the puzzle of what spooked Arthur so badly. She knew as little as Charles.

Charles, of course, was not pleased with knowing so little. It messed with the way he organized the world. He had to figure out how things worked, trace the patterns and connections. He did not do well with mysteries, and Thom was worried that it was too much strain on a fevered brain.

"What about Houdini?" Charles said, lying on his stomach on his narrow bed, arm draped over the side to trace the wood grains in the floor.

"What about him?" Thom leaned his forehead against the window, his mind on the woefully out-of-tune piano downstairs. In New York they had a man, blind but with a perfect ear, who came round to tune their piano once a month. He'd asked Mrs. Johnson, but no one in town knew how. Maybe he could figure it out. Without music, everything felt so real, so airless.

"You remember what Houdini did when we saw him! If he can break out of chains, surely this Mary woman could have faked her own death. What if she used a harness!"

Thom raised a dark eyebrow. "Did it look like she had much room for a harness beneath what she was wearing?"

Charles blushed. "Well, but something like that."

"And she put on the show knowing we'd be there at that exact time?"

"I don't know! What else makes sense?"

Thom's fingers sighed into a sonata against the rippled glass. "Arthur knows something. I wish he'd quit disappearing."

"You could always follow him up the side of the house in the middle of the night." Charles looked smug at his brother's surprised expression. "There are benefits to being a light sleeper, and sharing a room with your dreadful snoring. I've seen him, every night this week, scaling the wall straight up."

"Where is he going?" Thom briefly had an image of Arthur sneaking into Cora's room. It filled him with a flare of jealousy . . . but certainly Cora didn't seem the type to entertain those kinds of affections. Especially not if Arthur were related to them, though Thom couldn't see any resemblance, and the story Charles had gotten from Minnie was entirely speculation on her part.

"He stays up on the roof, I think. Comes back down around dawn. Our housemate is a very odd sort of fellow."

"Indeed."

"Your fingers are driving me insane. Go play the piano. Oh! Better yet, go and find me some fresh fruit. Mrs. Johnson's preserves are so sticky sweet they give me a headache. I promise to nap like a good invalid while you're gone, and then I promise to feel so well we can finally get out of this blasted room."

"Deal." Mussing his brother's hair as he walked by, Thom tightened his tie and took the stairs two at a time. He passed no one on his way out, and was soon in the middle of the main street of the town. Overpriced stalls to tempt summer vacationers were placed outside along the walkways. Doubtless there was a way to buy things for less money, but he didn't care. If he had to pay twice what the fruit was worth, he'd do so happily both for his brother and for being outside.

"And would you like a basket to carry everything in?" The woman, mid-thirties but pretty in a solid, healthy way, leaned forward. "It'll look so much nicer."

Laughing at being conned by a small-town woman, Thom went along with it. "Well, of course. Can't have fruit without the basket." Beaming triumphantly, the woman loaded the basket with apples in the bottom and strawberries on top. The strawberries looked a bit anemic — still not the best time for them — but they'd do just fine. And he could give the basket to Mrs. Johnson as a gift. Charles was always telling him to pay more attention to details when it came to women.

Something in the low, cheerful hum of sidewalk noise triggered an instant unease, making his stomach tighten. Looking up sharply, Thom handed his money to the woman and tried to identify what was bothering him.

He couldn't see anything amiss and tried to shrug the sensation away. Biting into an apple, he walked slowly along, glancing through store windows to see if anything else might make Charles happy. He saw some ribbons that reminded him of the ones Minnie used to hold her hair back, and wondered if it would be too forward to buy some for the sisters.

He felt guilty for his role in that night, and what a toll it had taken on everyone. Some ribbons might be just the thing. . . .

As he opened the door, a jingling bell matched the tone of voice of a woman talking. ". . . just this week. Yes, the cottage on the bay. Very lovely. And you can deliver?"

The instinct to hide was sudden and overpowering. Thom ducked behind shelves displaying cookware, trying to place the voice and figure out why it affected him so.

"Of course!" the shop worker answered, his young voice stretched and cracked by recent growth. "Anything you need. If we don't carry it, I'll get it somewhere else."

"There's a good boy," the woman said, and everything snapped into place. He *knew* her voice. She was the woman who had scared his father.

What was she doing here?

His father had sent them here the day after talking with her. And for her to be here, too? The world was not such a small place for something like this to be coincidence.

Squaring his shoulders and standing straight, Thom came around the corner as casually as he could. He'd see who she was without her noticing him. Looking up from a set of china, Thom found himself facing her.

She smiled, full red lips not showing her teeth. Her hair was dark and pinned back beneath an elegant hat. She stood nearly as tall as him, but there was something in her bearing and the way she held eye contact that made him feel smaller.

"Hello," she said, amusement pulling the corners of her mouth. "Shopping?"

"I — no, I — well, yes," Thom stuttered.

She took an apple from his basket, tucking it into her bag. "Pick out something nice for your brother," she said, teeth finally showing.

Thom watched, speechless, as she swept out of the shop and away.

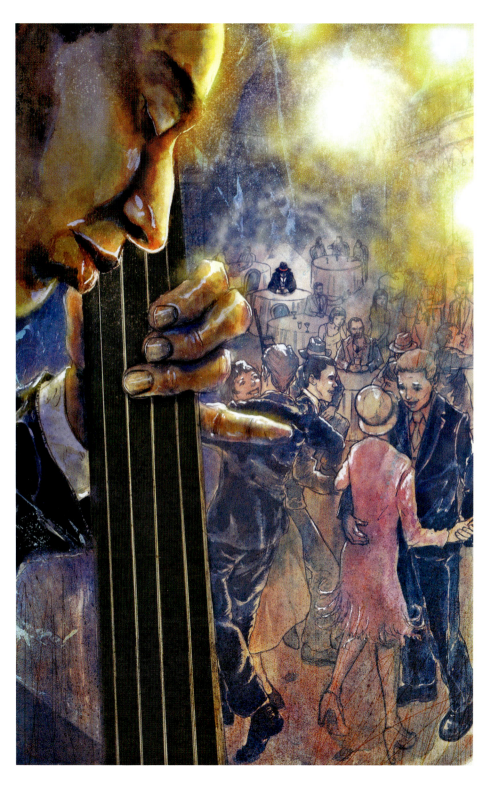

NINE

CHARLES SAT NEXT TO THOM, ON THE BANKS OF A STREAM HIDDEN BEHIND THE TOWN IN A TALL COPSE OF TREES. It was a cold clear singing dream of a creek, and he did not miss New York a bit. Cora and Minnie were here, they were his for the summer, and he took that gift very seriously.

As Minnie finished her dramatic reading of *The Rime of the Ancient Mariner*, Cora triumphantly pulled Charles's straw boating hat from the large picnic basket she had packed this morning. "Here you are! I had a feeling you'd be wanting it."

He took it with a grateful exclamation, and Cora didn't see the secret sly happiness to his thanks. Thom had everything wrong. He'd tried to tiptoe around Cora after that horribly wonderful night with the witch, but what a girl like her required was to be *needed*. In the six days since that incident, Charles had made a game of forgetting things, or requesting things, or otherwise being ridiculous. Cora was far more cheerful when she thought she was being useful.

Minnie was harder than Cora, which was why Charles liked her more. He'd think he had her figured out, only to lose her attention to a far-off gaze or a discontented sigh.

He missed the challenge of seeing problems and inventing ways to fix them. He'd been invaluable to his father last year, before he got sick, knowing he'd take over the business and spare Thom the agony of a trade his mind was incompatible with. Ah, sad fates! If only Charles could find a way around this truncation of his own future.

No matter. All machines wore out with time, and the human body was no different. In the meantime, he'd figure out how to spin dreamy Minnie closer to him. He was determined to have a kiss from her before too long.

Charles lay back on the picnic blanket, crossing his hands behind his head to stare up at the blue sky fighting through the lacework of branches. He was quite satisfied with the elements of this summer and how they were working together. And when he got melancholy, the ocean was constant and endless enough to swallow up any notions of human significance.

The only disappointment was his mystery, Arthur. Charles had been primed for more adventure, but Arthur denied them. Right now he slept, propped up in the concave curve of a large tree trunk, cradled by the roots so that he looked like something out of one of Minnie's fairy stories.

"Does he ever do anything but nap?" Charles wondered aloud. He had hoped Arthur would be dark and brooding like the anti-hero of *Wuthering Heights*, which he was reading at Minnie's insistence. But other than the odd bantering joke with Minnie or Cora, he was silent and forgettable.

Cora's eyes clouded with worry. "I think he must be ill."

"Or cursed!" Minnie watched Arthur, an unreadable play of emotions flitting across her features. "We did spy on a witch, after all. Maybe she's stealing his life away, bit by bit, to cheat death and sneak back into the world!"

Cora looked up sharply, surprising Charles. She usually dismissed Minnie's stories, but this one seemed to spook her.

"Or maybe he climbs on top of the roof and sits up there all night, every night," Thom said, raising an eyebrow (another reason Charles was sure to catch a kiss before him, as smiles sang to other lips in a way annoyed eyebrows never could).

"You've seen him?" Minnie glared at Thom, then at Arthur. Secrets! A sense of triumph flooded Charles as he found the key to Minnie. He'd go out of his way to tell her things he had never told anyone, wrap her in confidences until she was his. Doubtless before long he would run out of honest secrets and have to start inventing them, but when it came to Minnie, he didn't think she would mind.

"He's been up there every night since we went out. Question is, why?"

"None of your concern," Arthur said, startling everyone. He hadn't so much as twitched in an hour, and his eyes were still closed.

Cora abandoned the basket and walked over to kneel next to him. Her hand flitted over his forehead, not quite touching him, then went to her skirt pocket. "Are you having trouble sleeping?"

Arthur cracked open one eye and smiled at her. "Usually."

"Why the roof, though?" Thom asked.

"Why not?"

Minnie stood with a scowl, brushing away the leaves and dirt clinging to her skirt. She had refused to sit on the blanket, making tiny homes for fairies out of rocks and leaves instead. "The *top* of the roof? And you haven't invited me?"

"That's not safe," Cora said.

"But it's safe for Arthur?"

"What Arthur does is his business."

"But what I do is yours?"

"Strawberries!" Charles said, standing.

Minnie's scowl melted in confusion. "Strawberries?"

"Do you think they'll have any today? It's Market Day down by the pier, isn't it? I'd love some strawberries."

"Don't be silly," Cora answered, standing to fold the blanket and tuck it into the basket. "Market Day is overpriced nonsense for the tourists. If you want strawberries, we'll go through John. He'll do us fair."

Charles knew she'd say that, of course. They'd already had this discussion when Thom had come back with a basket of fruit two days prior. But Cora was no longer arguing with Minnie, because now she had a task. And both sisters had forgotten about Arthur. The way Minnie studied the older boy, Charles suspected he was the source of her far-off, troubled gazes. Diverting her attentions from Arthur was also essential to his quest for a kiss.

"Yes, let's avoid the market," Thom said, shuffling his feet and dodging Charles's eyes with an odd intensity. Come to think of it, Thom had been in a strange mood when he came back with that silly basket of fruit. Charles had thought it merely worry for his health, but maybe it was something else entirely.

"The old church is on the way. It's haunted," Minnie said, with the same reverent sweetness another girl might comment on the stained-glass windows or historic steeple.

"Perfect!" Charles held out his elbow to her, noting with pleasure when Arthur drifted behind them.

The chapel was a narrow white building, too small for the town but lovingly maintained. Its steeple, domed and adorned with a simple iron cross, had been saved when the previous chapel burned down nearly a century ago. Rising two stories above the single-story building, it was a landmark everyone used to navigate around the flat seaside curve of the town center. There was nowhere worth going that couldn't be found via the cross, as Mrs. Johnson was fond of saying.

Charles found the interior to be like the inside of most houses of worship — dark and smelling of age, the pews worn with the weight of desperate faith and tedious complacence. He'd often wondered how, exactly, one's prayers were supposed to make it through so much dim, dusty space between the heart and the ceiling.

Many people invoked God when finding out about his condition, but Charles didn't much care either way. If God wanted to cut his life short, God would have to worry about what to do with him afterward. It wasn't any of Charles's concern. When he was younger he had figured out that there was no way to fit faith into the workings of his everyday life in a way that made sense, and so he had shifted religion to the side as a useless extra part.

Thom walked in past the pews and straight to the small organ, tucked into the wall beneath a carved arch. Cora sat at the edge of a pew with her hands folded sedately in her lap, while Minnie prowled up and down the center aisle before noticing Thom sit down on the organ bench and run his fingers lovingly along the keys.

"Can you play?" she asked.

Thom sighed, silently fingering notes. "Mostly the piano, though I can play the organ, too. I miss it like breathing."

"So that's what you're always doing with your fingers." Cora tapped her own in imitation. If she'd noticed that, maybe Thom had a chance at a summer kiss of his own. Charles needed to decide whether he wanted to help his brother in that regard.

Minnie sat next to Thom on the bench. "Play something!"

Thom's feet worked the pedals and the first few notes of "All Creatures of Our God and King" tumbled out, lifting along the rafters and pushing aside the weight of dust and dim. Some of the tightness left Charles's chest. He did not know how to fix the holes his absence would leave for Thom, but he hoped music would help.

"Boring!" Minnie said. "Do you only know hymns?"

Grinning mischievously, Thom's well-trained fingers transitioned immediately into a ragtime piece. Not "Maple Leaf Rag," as none of them would ever again be able to hear that song without dreadful associations, but another fast, rowdy, joyous tune.

Minnie squealed with delight, standing and twirling through the church to the closed front door, where Arthur leaned in the shadows. "Dance with me!"

The line between Cora's brows appeared. "Perhaps this isn't appropriate for a church?"

Minnie spun by, dragging Arthur with her. Charles cursed his lack of breath. The walk here had cost him already, though he tried to hide it.

"Don't be sour, Cora," Minnie said. "How could God hate anything that makes your heart feel like dancing?"

Charles nudged Cora with his shoulder, forcing her to look at him as he gave her his most winning grin. He knew the full impact of his large hazel eyes, as well as Cora's proprietary desire to make him happy. She shook her head and darted nervous glances back to the door, but her brow relaxed. She even began to tap her foot.

Thom's fingers flew over the keys, building up to the end of the song, when a fist banged against the front door of the church, causing him to stop. Their ears rang with the missing notes.

The door rattled, catching against the bolt.

"Locked it," Arthur said with a shrug, stopping Minnie midtwirl. His hands lingered at her waist, and Minnie flushed. "Out the side."

Cora stood with a low moan of despair or fear, but Minnie and Thom shrieked with laughter, following Arthur past the pulpit and into the dark corner at the front where a small door led to a tiny, closet-like study. Charles and Cora brought up the rear, and together the five tumbled out of the study into the fast-fading day.

"This way," Arthur said, turning down a side street and taking them on a winding, circuitous route through the town. Minnie took Charles's arm; she was nearly as breathless as he was, glancing constantly over her shoulder for pursuit. Charles was too happy that she had chosen *his* arm to care very much whether they were caught.

An angry shout tumbled between houses after them.

"Charles can't run much longer!" Thom said, puncturing Charles's mood. Though Charles *was* hoping they'd be caught very soon. He could feel his heart, ragged and rebelling against this strain, no matter how pretty the girl at his side.

Arthur nodded toward a row of houses. "Minnie, hide with him. We'll keep the chase going."

Tugging his hand, Minnie pulled him through a narrow gap between fences and into an overgrown yard with an old wooden swing. They ducked low, letting the strands of grass tickle their cheeks.

"I'm so glad you came this summer," Minnie whispered, eyes shining with her own brand of fierce delight.

Charles ignored the painful twists in his chest and the loss of sensation in his hands. "I am, too. Can I tell you a secret?"

Her eyes lit up even brighter. "Yes!"

Smiling slyly, Charles leaned closer. "It's a very big secret. I'll have to whisper it in your mouth."

Just as understanding wrote its way onto Minnie's face, Charles pressed his lips against hers. Kissing Minnie was like laughter, light and joyful and utterly lacking in guile.

As soon as she pulled away, grinning and pushing his shoulder in playful reproach, Charles was already plotting how he could do it again. As Minnie peeked through the fence to see if they were free, Charles looked toward the house.

A bearded man stood in front of a large window, barely visible through the summer sunshine. He was watching them, smiling, but Charles felt no warmth.

"Who lives here?" Charles whispered.

Minnie didn't turn around. "No one. It's always empty. Let's go!"

Charles didn't take his eyes off the man until he and Minnie were safely through the fence, but he could feel the weight of his gaze all the way home.

BOSTON, MASSACHUSETTS, 1926

ST. GYM

RICHMOND, VIRGINIA, 1928

TAMPA, FLORIDA, 1929

HATTIESBURG, MISSISSIPPI, 1930

PRAGUE, 1931

SOFIA, BULGARIA, 1933

CAPPADOCIA, TURKEY, 1935

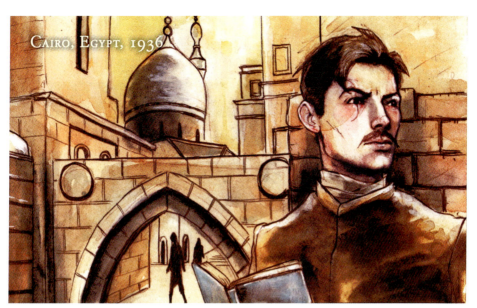

CAIRO, EGYPT, 1936

DECEMBER, 1941

TEN

Minnie upended the entire jug of seawater onto Cora's head. As her sister sputtered, Minnie put her hands on her hips and said, "Well, now you're wet, anyway. May as well swim."

Cora shrieked in rage and stood, chasing Minnie down the rocky beach. Minnie darted left, into the breaking waves, sure she'd be free. To her shock and delight, Cora followed, plunging into the water after her. Minnie "tripped," falling forward in front of Cora, who pushed Minnie's head under an obliging wave before helping her to her feet. They were both chest-deep now, the water bitingly cold.

Cora's eyes blazed with rage, but then turned up at the corner, and before she could catch herself, she was laughing. Minnie threw her arms around her sister's waist, using the water's buoyancy to lift her up in a hug.

"Race you to the rocks!"

Cora hesitated, turning back toward the shore where the boys looked on, bemused, dry and comfortable if a bit too hot. Then she reached down, pulled off her shoes, and flung them onto the beach. One hit Thomas's shin, and Minnie thought he looked decidedly pleased.

Without warning, Cora dove forward, pulling herself through the waves with the strong strokes their father taught them.

"Cheater!" Minnie laughed, taking off after her but knowing she'd never catch up. She didn't mind.

When they got to the rocks that marked the edge of the

narrow, sheltered cove beach, they clung to them, breathing hard and blinking salt water out of their eyes.

"Thomas fancies you," Minnie said.

Cora sputtered, and it wasn't because she had swallowed water. "He's very kind. But I don't think —"

"Oh, he absolutely does. Don't be coy. Do you like him? I think he's nice. Too serious by half, but he's handsome enough. Devastatingly so when he's playing music, don't you think?"

It had been three days since they had observed Thomas's transcendent time at the organ. Even Minnie had fancied him when he was playing, and Cora's flushed cheeks turned a deeper red at the memory. Minnie leaned forward, throwing one cold arm around Cora's neck. "I'm so happy. Right now, I'm the happiest girl alive."

"You always exaggerate," Cora chided, but she sounded happy, too. "What about you? I think Charles likes you."

"Oh, he's mad for me. He kissed me."

"Minnie! You let him?"

"I've kissed every other boy in town." Her eyes found their way automatically to Arthur, standing with his toes nearly in the water, watching them. Not *every* other boy. Not her favorite, her best, her secret.

"Honestly, you need to be more careful. A girl's reputation is —"

"It was just a kiss, Cora. Kisses are like candy. Everyone should be able to enjoy them, and no one should take them seriously. Charles is a doll, and if it makes him happy to kiss me and me happy to kiss him, where's the harm?"

"If things turn sour . . . We need the money. We can't afford to lose them as boarders."

Minnie rolled her eyes, then splashed water at Cora. "They aren't going anywhere until the summer ends."

Minnie looked at Arthur again, and this time she wasn't secret enough to avoid being caught at it by Cora.

"Oh, Min," Cora said, her voice soft and sad. "You —"

"I what?" Minnie's voice was falsely bright, her smile painful.

"I don't want you to get hurt. Just remember that some things can't happen." She gave Minnie a significant look, then shrugged so they could both pretend they didn't know what they were referring to. "Remember that Charles is sick. Just be careful, okay?"

Climbing up onto the rock where they used to sun themselves and pretend to be mermaids, Minnie spun with her arms lifted above her head. "Never!" she shouted, jumping into the water.

When they finally slogged back onto the beach, waterlogged and freezing, Minnie could tell that Cora already regretted this relapse. Taking the picnic blanket, Minnie wrapped it around Cora's shoulders, leaving an arm around her waist and whispering nonsense to her as they walked home. If she clung to her sister, if she held her tightly enough, she'd be able to get her back.

"You boys go in the front," Minnie said as they drew close. "Distract our mother."

"You mean she doesn't like you two to go swimming in the ocean in your clothes?" Charles asked, teasing.

"Oh, no, any mother approves of that. It's the hair she'll be upset about." Minnie held up a tangled strand of dark curls.

"Go on," Thomas said. "We'll ask her to make us some food. She thinks we're constantly on the verge of starvation."

"You're a peach! Come on, Cora." They broke off, sneaking toward the back of the house and through the veranda. Waiting a couple of minutes, they slipped out of their shoes again, tiptoeing through the hall to the narrow set of servant's stairs hidden in the back of the house, lit only by a small, circular window. Their stockings left wet prints as they walked.

Minnie cracked open the door to the second floor, checking that the coast was clear before waving Cora forward. They were just making their way to their room when a throat cleared behind them.

Squeaking, both girls turned around to find themselves face-to-face with one of the boarders. It was the man, the one with the mustache and silver streak in his hair. Minnie could never decide if he was handsome or frightening — his face was angled and his eyes just so that they walked the line of being too unusual to be plain but too odd to be beautiful.

"Well, what have we here?" he asked. "Did you two fall in the wash?"

Cora deflected. "Can I help you with something, Mr. . . ."

"Alden. Just Alden. It looks as though you two have been for a swim. Would your mother be happy with that, I wonder? Two girls, swimming in their clothes, doubtless in the company of those boys always lurking about here."

Minnie scowled, but he didn't notice. He hadn't taken his eyes off of Cora. Minnie was suddenly glad Cora was the one wrapped up in a blanket.

Cora bit her lip. "It was an accident. We were just going to get cleaned up."

"Of course. No need to worry. I won't tell your mother." His smile got sharper, and it touched his eyes but in a way that made them seem even less friendly. "I do like being owed a favor by a pretty girl."

Minnie opened her mouth to protest, but Cora stood straight and regarded Alden with a cool, level gaze. "Sir, I trust my mother's anger far more than favors from men I do not know. I have no desire to be beholden to you for anything other than a comfortable stay in a pleasant home for the summer, the same as we offer all our guests."

Minnie expected him to be outraged, but if anything, he looked delighted. "I see. Good day, Cora." He didn't move, standing a breath too close, as Cora fished the key out of her pocket and opened their bedroom door. When Minnie slammed it shut behind them, he was still in the hall, watching.

"He is so creepy," Minnie hissed.

"Hush. It's fine." Cora paced, hands immediately going to worry the stone she always kept in her pocket. The blood drained from her face as her pocket turned out to be empty. "No," she moaned, searching again. "I didn't take it out before we went in the water!"

Minnie frowned. "It's just a stone."

Tears pooled in Cora's eyes, and she kept feeling her dress as though the stone would magically turn up. "No, it's not. Father gave it to me the day before he . . ." She burst into sobs, sitting heavily on the bed.

"Oh, Cora." Minnie fought back tears of her own. It was her fault, for dragging Cora into the water. It was always her fault. "We can go back, look for it, and —"

Cora laughed, but it sounded harsh beneath her tears. "Yes, let's look for a beach rock on the beach. Never mind. It's silly. I shall simply worry less."

"It's not silly," Minnie whispered.

Cora shook her head, shutting Minnie out again. "That man. Do you think he'll tell Mother?"

"No. I don't." He had nothing to gain by it, and it struck Minnie that Alden was a man who always wanted something to gain.

And it didn't fail to register for her that he had no reason to be in this hallway — in the back of the house, where the family had their rooms and no guests ever stayed.

Minnie wanted to stay and comfort Cora, but it was clear Cora wanted no such thing. Very well, then. Minnie tore out of her clothes, throwing on a change of dress and pulling her hair back, not caring that it soaked her collar. "I'm going to go get something to eat," she said, ducking out of the room before Cora could protest being left with all the wet clothes. Minnie took the back stairs, slipping along the wall and into the pantry. She found the kitchen empty, and slid a small, sharp knife out of the drawer.

She could not shake the way that man had leered at her sister. Like Cora was already his.

Cora was *hers*. She would never lose her, and she would never let anyone hurt her again. A spare ribbon secured the knife under her dress against her thigh, and the cold secret of it felt like power.

ELEVEN

CORA WALKED NEXT TO THOMAS — BUT NOT SO CLOSE THAT THEY WERE TOUCHING — DOWN THE LONG LANE TOWARD TOWN. They had left Minnie and Charles engaged in a game of checkers, where Minnie was cheating outrageously and Charles was letting her.

The bright summer day filled in the silence with a thousand small sounds of life, but Cora wanted to talk with Thomas. She was still humiliated from her hysterics that night on Barley Hill. So what if she'd seen a figure looking down at her from the second story? Arthur had explained that he'd gone upstairs to look for Mary and glanced down to check on her.

And she'd fainted. And Thomas had carried her home. She blushed deeply just thinking about it and, struck with the irrational fear that Thomas was thinking about the exact thing, rushed to fill the silence. "Do you have the list for the chemist? He tends to forget things unless he has it in writing."

"Yes." He pulled a slip out of his pocket. His handwriting was neat, slanted letters. There was an ink stain on his middle finger that she realized was always there.

"Do you write? Music, I mean. You play so well."

The corners of his lips turned down, but his eyes crinkled up and she was sure he was trying not to betray his delight. "I try, here and there. It's rubbish."

"I'd like to hear it sometime."

"Really?" He turned toward her, hazel eyes filled with such honest hope she realized how deliberately careful nearly all of his expressions were. Not guarded and secretive, like Arthur, but . . . shielded. As though he was afraid of ever feeling what he actually felt, of putting on anything other than a brave, practical face.

He was terrified all the time.

Her heart fluttered with the recognition of someone else who understood what it was to forever try to be strong and constantly come up short.

"Really," she said, her voice as gentle as her smile. She hesitated, then, before she could think better of it, put her hand in the crook of his elbow. "I'll make certain Mr. Clemens follows the order to the letter. He hates vacationers, but he's always liked Mother very much. We'll get exactly what Charles needs."

"Thank you," Thomas said, reaching up to adjust his hat, then his tie, then his collar. Cora felt a flush of something that felt suspiciously like pride. She had the power to fluster him with such a simple action as her hand on his arm!

They walked like that to the town. The cool, dim interior of the chemist's shop was welcome after the heat of the afternoon. She gave Mr. Clemens the instructions, and they watched as he pulled out powders and liquids, muttering to himself as he mixed several packets and a couple of glass vials. In a few minutes he had everything together and helped Cora pack it all carefully into her basket.

"How sick is he?" he asked, looking up through his bushy gray eyebrows at Thomas.

Thomas cleared his throat, avoiding Cora's concerned gaze. "Getting better every day."

"Hmm." Mr. Clemens scowled doubtfully, then calculated the cost and counted out Thomas's change.

Cora fretted over the shift in Thomas's demeanor. She knew Charles was sick — very sick — and Mr. Clemens's tone made her think that it was not a sickness to be recovered from. They would do all they could for him, but right now Cora worried more about the older brother. It was not easy to be sick, surely, but it was also not easy to be powerless to help those you loved.

"Does he need any of this right now?" she asked. "Because if it can wait, I have been meaning to visit Miss Smith's candy shop. I can never go with Minnie because she spends all our pocket change, but the candy dishes at the boardinghouse are getting low. And," she added, whispering conspiratorially, "my personal stockpile of sweets is nearly out."

"Well, we can't have that, now, can we?" He offered his elbow and she gladly took it. "We could even bring some back for Charles and Minnie."

"If you insist on being noble and generous, I suppose we can share. But most of it will be our secret." Cora noted that Thomas's face grew even brighter at her choice of pronoun.

Perhaps Minnie ought to be cautioning me *about the wisdom of falling for summer boarders.*

"Tell me about New York," Cora said as they turned the corner onto the main street.

"It's —" Thomas froze, then, without warning, pulled Cora back around the building. "That woman — she's just outside the grocer's — do you know her?"

Frowning, Cora peered around the corner. There was a tall woman, hair dark and dress elegant and obviously expensive. Cora knew every yearlong resident, and recognized most of the regular summer visitors, but had never seen this woman before.

"No, I don't," she whispered, still observing. "Why?"

"I ran into her the other day. And I think . . ." Thomas paused, then rushed out the next sentence as though embarrassed by it. "I think she followed us here. I heard her, the night before we left, speaking with my father. And she knew I had a brother when I saw her, though we've never met."

Cora frowned, unable to determine why Thomas seemed so spooked to run into an acquaintance of his father's. Then the woman turned and, in an exasperated twist of her shoulders, motioned for someone to come closer.

That was when Cora noticed another woman clinging to the shadows of a door stoop, her dress oddly childlike and several years out of fashion. Her hair draped across her collar and down to her knees in an impossibly long braid.

The witch.

"Thomas!" Cora gasped. He was immediately by her side, and recognition dawned on his face with the same mixture of surprise and horror.

The elegant woman spoke to Mary, reaching up to tuck a strand of hair back in the braid. Then she took Mary's hand, patted it, and pulled Mary alongside her.

"She's rather upright for a dead woman," Thomas said, his voice dry. Cora didn't know whether to be relieved at this proof of life, or cross at the witch for pulling such a horrible trick on all of them.

"They know each other," Cora said. "No one knows the witch — Mary, I mean. She never comes out of her house. Why would she now?"

"Let's follow them."

Cora hesitated, but found the pull of answers too strong to resist. She felt as though Mary owed her. She'd spent too long being terrified of everything she associated with that house and that woman, and now to see her walking down the street as though everything were normal? Cora wouldn't have it. This was her town.

They hurried after the women, keeping a discreet distance but careful not to lose them. Mary drifted as she walked, constantly pulled back to the sidewalk and redirected by the other woman.

They disappeared around a corner. Turning it, Cora and Thomas pulled up short, horrified to be nearly on top of their prey. They ducked behind a shrub, peering through the branches. Mary and her friend were outside a small, expensive teahouse Cora had never visited.

"There you are," said a man — Alden! — joining them. "Constance, you are as lovely as a dream. And, Mary, pet, how wonderful to see you again after all these years." He leaned forward and Cora could have sworn Mary *hissed* at him.

When all three had disappeared into the teahouse, Cora and Thomas briefly whispered about whether to follow them in, but decided it couldn't be done unobserved. They walked quickly back in the direction of home.

"Isn't that the man staying at the boardinghouse?" Thomas asked.

"It is." Cora frowned, fighting back a shudder. "I don't like him. I think he was waiting for me the other day, in our hall where he had no business to be."

"I don't like any of them. And it can't be a coincidence that they know each other. That woman — Constance — showing up here after I heard her threatening my father? Alden staying at the boardinghouse with us? And then that crazy witch."

"She couldn't have known we'd be at her house, though," Cora said, trying to puzzle it out.

"She could have, if Alden watched us leave and then ran ahead and told her."

"But why would they be watching us?"

Thomas scowled and kicked at a stone as they left the sidewalk for the dirt lane to the house. "My father is wealthy. Very wealthy.

The way he was talking that night — he was scared. He's not a man who gets scared. Maybe he sent us away so we'd be safe from that woman, but now she's followed us here!"

Cora's head spun. "Do you think they want to kidnap you?"

"Or Charles. Or maybe she's blackmailing my father. I don't know."

"Do you think you ought to leave? If she knows where you are . . ."

"I'll send a wire to my father. She knows where we live at home, too, so going back there wouldn't solve the problem. I want to keep it from Charles, but it's probably safer if everyone is on guard. We'll talk with them about it. Besides, if Constance hasn't done anything yet, we're probably safe for the time being. Right?"

Cora couldn't find it in herself to agree. Nothing felt safe in her town anymore.

LAS VEGAS, NEVADA
OCTOBER, 1948

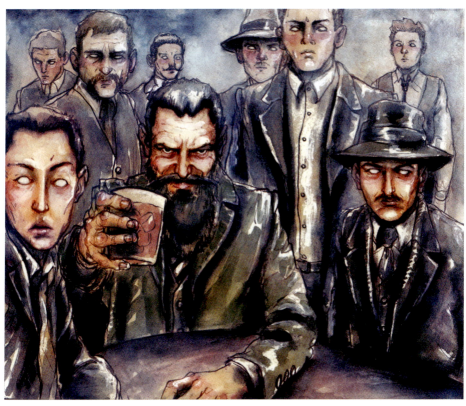

TWELVE

ARTHUR NEEDED TO GET RID OF THOMAS AND CHARLES. It was either that, or run away. Arthur could not bear the thought of leaving Cora and Minnie behind, nor could he devise a way to convince them to run with him.

But it was very clear to him now that whatever forces were converging on this town, Thomas and Charles were already tangled. He would not let Minnie and Cora be caught as well.

He paced in his small attic room, a path well worn by his feet. Dust motes hung lazily in the golden patches of dawn's new light, eddying and resettling every time he disturbed them.

The case called to him from its grave. There were lists in there, connections his father had made. His mother kept the lists tacked up, read them to herself. Mostly it was places but also names, and he had a creeping suspicion that if he were to look he would find Wolcott among them. But if he opened the case, if he read what was in there, who was to say he wouldn't catch the same obsession that had orphaned him?

No. It was bad luck for Charles and Thomas, and he was sorry for them, but he would not give up what he had here to try and save them.

They would have to save themselves.

With a weary sigh, he pulled the unopened letters he'd stolen from Mary's house out from beneath his pillow. Tapping on the aged, thick paper of the envelopes, his fingers hovered, and then he tucked them back away. He'd burn them tonight, rid himself of this link, and then convince Mrs. Johnson to send Charles and Thomas away.

Arthur's jaw tightened. It wasn't because he was jealous of losing so much of the girls' attentions — it *wasn't*. He had seen it in Cora, but it did not bother him because she seemed genuinely happy. Minnie, however. He had seen her, more and more, with something desperate but determined in her face as she looked away from him and to Charles.

He couldn't lose her.

Them. He couldn't lose them. He had to protect them. His life before them had been controlled by fear, but the day he decided to stay, they became the foundation of his world.

He walked silently down the narrow wooden stairs to the second floor, passing the girls' room and pausing, as was his habit, to listen for their soft sleeping murmurings and make sure that everything sounded as it should.

Satisfied, he went to the kitchen, unlocking it with his key. He'd eat before anyone else was awake. He could go sleep for a couple of hours after, knowing the girls were safe in their morning chores. His body ached from holding its rigid sentinel position on the peak of the roof yet again, and he felt the sort of bone-weary tired he hadn't since losing his mother.

All his vigilance haunted him, though. If one of *them* was under the very roof he was watching from, how could he possibly see everything he needed to?

He cut a chunk of yesterday's bread, smearing some of Mrs. Johnson's strawberry preserves on it. He wanted something weightier but was too tired to prepare anything. Turning to go back to bed, he nearly ran into Thomas.

"What are you doing in here?" Thomas asked.

Arthur raised an eyebrow. "The kitchen is off-limits to guests. I am not a guest."

Thomas's shoulder stooped, then he straightened deliberately. "Mrs. Johnson told me I was welcome to get whatever I needed, whenever I needed it. I'm making tea."

The dark circles under Thomas's eyes told a story of more than one sleepless night. With a sympathetic pang, Arthur wondered if perhaps Thomas kept his own nightly vigil over his brother.

"Tea is in the pantry. Here, I'll show you." Turning, Arthur opened the door and felt for the jars by memory.

They both heard footsteps outside the kitchen. Without thinking, Arthur grabbed Thomas and pulled him into the pantry, closing the door so only a sliver remained for them to see out of.

"What?" Thomas whispered.

"No one should be down here yet." Arthur was suddenly embarrassed at this display. His first reaction was always to hide, to watch unseen. He had no way to justify it to Thomas. Cringing, he planned how to play it off as a sort of game.

Then the door opened and Alden came in.

Both boys held their breath, not daring to so much as breathe. Alden walked to the wall next to a bright window, where a small board Arthur had made hung. It held keys to every room in the house, neatly labeled in Cora's precise handwriting. It had been a Christmas gift for Mrs. Johnson, who was forever fumbling for the right key or misplacing spares.

The kitchen was locked all the time unless the cook or Mrs. Johnson were in here.

Except when Arthur opened it this morning and neglected to lock it behind himself.

Reaching up, Alden slipped the key to Cora and Minnie's room free, replacing it with his own similar-looking one. He tucked the key into his jacket pocket, humming softly to himself, and slid back out of the kitchen.

"Did he just take the key I think he took?" Thomas whispered.

Arthur pushed out past him, taking Alden's key off the hook and putting his own kitchen key in its place. Thomas followed him out into the hall.

"Where are you going?"

"To sit in front of Cora and Minnie's room until they wake up."

"But what are we going to do about Alden? He has their key now!"

Arthur's face darkened. "We steal it back."

Thomas suggested a game of croquet on the front lawn that day. Charles sat in a chair, a blanket over his legs as he cheered Minnie on. Cora chided Minnie for cheating and complimented Thomas on his form. Arthur leaned in a shadow against the side of the house, watching the front door.

He waited.

Sometime after Mrs. Johnson brought them lemonade, Alden strode out, tipping his hat with an oily smile at Cora, then walking toward town.

The second he disappeared around the bend, Arthur was inside, headed for the guest wing. He leaned down in front of Alden's door, inserting the key.

It didn't work.

"He wouldn't have left his own key," Thomas said behind him, startling Arthur so badly he nearly fell over. "It would be too obvious that he was the one who'd taken the girls' key."

"Yes, *thank you*," Arthur hissed. He pulled out his picks and slid them into the keyhole.

"How long will this take?"

"I didn't invite you." The tools caught, and with an expert twist, Arthur was able to open the door.

"Can you teach me to do that?"

"No. Stand watch." Arthur crept into the room. It was sterile, perfectly clean, the bed with its creamy linens made up. The desk by the window was bare, chair pushed in, nothing left out. He opened the polished wood armoire. The bottom was lined with five identical pairs of shined shoes, and hanging were several well-tailored suits. He recognized the jacket from this morning and quickly searched the pockets.

The key wasn't there.

"Can you open this?"

Arthur turned to find Thomas crouched by the bed, a low wooden chest half-pulled out. Biting back an angry question on just what, exactly, Thomas thought standing watch meant, Arthur stalked over and examined the box. The lock was old, complicated but beautiful.

"It'll take a minute." His pick slid in, springs and catches felt by instinct and memory. Thomas stopped hovering and darted around the room, feeling under the pillow, behind the curtains, under the desk.

After far too long, Arthur's alarm growing every second, the lock finally gave. He paused, the latch's metal cool against his fingers.

He really, really did not want to know what was in this box.

"Go on, then," Thomas said, leaning over his shoulder.

Arthur lifted the lid.

Inside, nestled atop sheaves of paper, maps, and newspaper articles, were three necklaces, each with a gleaming green scarab beetle pendant.

Arthur closed his eyes. He'd known. Of course he'd known, since he'd seen one at Mary's house and discovered that Mary was connected to Alden. But he'd still hoped that it was all a mistake. Hoped that somehow this had nothing to do with his father's obsessions. Hoped that it really was about Thomas and Charles's money.

Hoped that there was still some way to stay.

"What does *Ladon Vitae* mean?" Thomas asked, pulling out a stack of thick, hand-lettered papers. "That's Latin, right? *Vitae* means 'life.' But what's *Ladon*?"

Arthur sat, shifting to the side, letting Thomas paw through the chest. It didn't matter. Nothing mattered anymore. His voice felt dead as it came out. "It was a dragon in Greek mythology." He had seen countless images of it, versions of the myth told to him as bedtime stories.

But there are no stories here. Only nightmares.

"I can't find the key . . . but this is all so strange. Drawings, maps, lists —" Thomas paused. "Arthur, look."

"I don't want to."

"Please."

The fear in the other boy's voice finally pulled Arthur's eyes up. He followed Thomas's finger to where he pointed at the name *Edward Wolcott*. Next to it was written: *Blood debt. Sacrifice required.*

"That's my father," Thomas whispered. "What does it mean?"

"It means you should take your brother and run."

"Why?" Thomas slipped the list into his pocket, then closed the chest. The latch would need to be relocked, but Arthur couldn't find the strength to care.

He stood and drifted to the door, pausing without looking back at Thomas. "Because if you don't hide, you'll die. You'll probably die, anyway."

Arthur walked back out to the front lawn, where Minnie and Cora laughed and played in the brilliant, safe sunshine.

Now all he had to do was figure out how to kidnap them both.

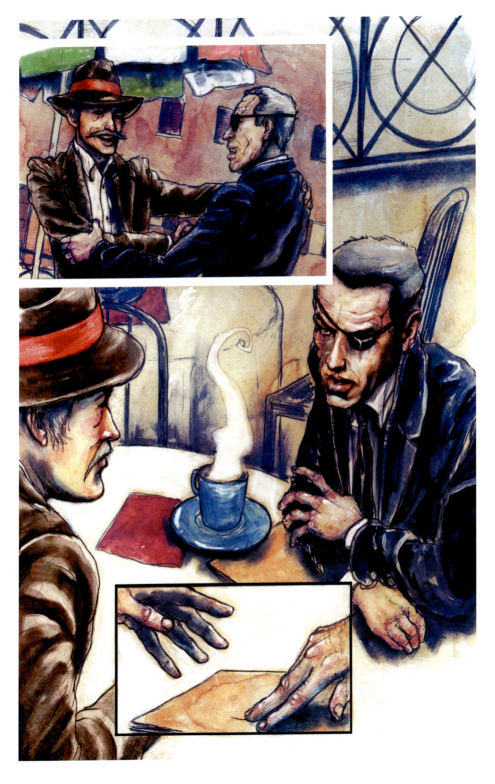

THIRTEEN

Thom burst into the bedroom, stopping short at the sight of Minnie peering into their window. She knocked. Charles's expression was delighted as he undid the latch and let the glass panes swing open on their hinges.

Thom, on the other hand, was annoyed. He needed to speak with Charles right now, and not with her here. He'd gone immediately to talk to Charles about what he'd found in Alden's room, only to be ambushed by Mrs. Humphrey and regaled with tales of her various medical maladies. She seemed to think because he was caring for his sick younger brother he had an intense fascination with all the ways a body can break. It was only by promising to play her favorite songs — Brahms, horrid, boring Brahms — that evening that Thom was finally able to break away.

And now Minnie was here.

"Won't you come in?" Charles asked, as though it were perfectly normal for a girl to come knocking at a second-story window.

"Of course not," Minnie said, sitting down with her feet hanging into the room, banging her stockinged heels against the wall. "It wouldn't be proper."

Charles laughed, then tried to stifle a cough that rattled through his chest like something had come unstuck in there. It hurt Thom to hear it.

Minnie pretended not to notice the cough. "Cora has gone to nap. Apparently when she gets the summer off, she doesn't know what to do with herself besides sleep. And I'm *not to bother you*, as she insisted Charles needed to be doing the same."

"He does," Thom said, trying to convey with an urgent expression and a jerk of his head that his brother needed to tell Minnie to leave.

Charles grinned, willfully ignoring him.

"You look as though you've seen a ghost, Thomas," Minnie said.

Thom paced a few steps, nervous energy too big for the room, then stopped and fixed his eyes on her. Well, if she was here, she'd have to answer his questions. "Just what exactly do you know about Arthur?"

Minnie narrowed her eyes suspiciously, shifting on the sill. Then she sniffed as though bored. "He's been with us a year. He knew my father."

It wasn't like Minnie not to tell an elaborate story when given the chance. Why was she hiding things? "Where did he live before? Who is his family? Come on, you have to know more."

"I *don't* know." Her face grew shadowed with something that looked like pain. "We think — we think he might be our half brother. From before Mother and Father married. Arthur knew our father, said that he would find them wherever they were living and bring them food and money. Anyway, it doesn't matter in the end. Arthur's ours." She sat up straighter, expression fierce. Thom glanced at Charles, wondering if he noticed the way she was when she talked about Arthur. His brother seemed calm, though.

"What's this about, Thom?" Charles asked, sitting on the edge of his bed and leaning against the wall.

Thom was torn. He wanted to protect Charles and keep any of this troubling information from him. But at the same time, how could Charles be safe if he didn't know there was danger?

Throwing his hands up in surrender, he turned the desk chair around and sat backward in it, resting his chin on its back. "That man staying here — Alden? We broke into his room."

Minnie jumped off the sill and came in, sitting next to Charles and listening intently. Thom continued to fill them in, culminating in the list he found with his father's name on it. "Obviously this group — Alden, that woman from New York, and the witch — have some sort of sinister plan that involves us."

Charles frowned thoughtfully. "There was a man I thought was watching us when we ran from the church. But he had a beard. It definitely wasn't Alden, and it certainly wasn't the woman you've described."

Minnie was *delighted*, which annoyed Thom as it was entirely the wrong reaction. "It could be a bigger conspiracy! But why did you break into Alden's room?" She tapped distractedly on her leg, playing with something beneath the fabric of her dress.

"We — Arthur and I — caught him stealing the key to your bedroom. We were trying to get it back."

Minnie's delighted expression turned sour and flat. "I'll tell my mother," she said, standing, hand now clutching something through her skirt. "She'll throw him out."

"There's more." Thomas's tone drove her to sit back down. "Arthur wouldn't answer my questions, but this group calls themselves the Ladon Vitae. And I think your *friend* knows all about them."

"Maybe he didn't really know anything. Arthur never gives straight answers."

Thom cut her with a well-practiced look. "He said that unless Charles and I run away right now, we'll be killed. And that we'll probably be killed regardless."

Minnie shrank back. "He might have been joking?"

"He wasn't. Either he's crazy, he's involved with them, or he has information I need to keep my brother safe."

Minnie's gaze darted to Charles and she softened. However she felt about Arthur, Thom could tell she cared about his brother, too.

"How can we get him to answer questions?" Charles asked, his face paler than usual.

"You can't," Minnie answered. "Believe me." She stood, hands tugging on the front of her blouse, then walked to the door. "Come on. My mother will know. It's time I asked her for the truth."

"Will she tell us, too?" Thom asked. He doubted very much that if Mrs. Johnson had kept Arthur's past a secret from her own daughters she'd be willing to release it for two new boarders.

Minnie rolled her eyes. "She won't know you're in the room, dummy."

After making tea and explaining that her mother would be in the kitchen in precisely three minutes, Minnie shut both boys in the pantry.

"I'm getting tired of this spot," Thom muttered.

"Oh, hello, Minnie," Mrs. Johnson said, right on time. "I didn't expect to find you in here. You girls haven't been inside much these days."

"No need to get the tea. I made it for you."

"Aren't you sweet! Thank you."

There was a creak as someone settled into a chair at the small, worn kitchen table, so unlike the polished one in the dining room.

"Mother, I need to know about Arthur."

There was a sputtering sound. "What do you mean?"

"I mean, I need to know about Arthur. We've never asked, and you've never told us, and I've tried to be respectful of that.

But I *need* to know: Is he my brother?" Her voice cracked with the emotional urgency of her question. Thom had to hand it to her — Minnie was a superb actress.

Mrs. Johnson started laughing, and for reasons Thom couldn't fathom, Minnie burst into gasping tears.

"Oh, sweetheart, I'm so sorry! But your brother? Whatever gave you that idea?"

"He knew Father! And you said he was family!"

"Come here, Min. I'm sorry. I wish you had asked me instead of assuming! I never talked about Arthur's past because it hurts me to think about, and I'm sure it hurts him, too. I'd hoped with a new start here we could help him heal from so much pain."

"But he's definitely not my brother," Minnie said, hiccupping.

Charles shifted next to Thom, something restless in his movements.

"No. His mother, Adelaide, was my best friend growing up. Together with your father we were inseparable. But then when we got older, and your father and I fell in love, Adelaide was pushed to the side. Then a young man came to town — a scholar — researching nonsense about ancient societies and conspiracies and evil. Adelaide was smitten with Josiah. He had an attractive, tragic air about him. I tried to warn her that no stable family could ever be built with such a strange, obsessive man, but she wouldn't hear it. In the end, your father and I didn't stop her from running off with him." Mrs. Johnson sighed heavily. "Josiah Liska was the death of her."

"What happened?" Minnie asked, voice still heavy with tears.

"They had a few good years. Traveling all the time, looking at 'sites' that held clues, visiting libraries. She wrote of Josiah's work and how important it was. They had a baby — Arthur —

but still never settled down. Her letters became increasingly erratic. Whatever Josiah thought he was discovering bled into every aspect of their lives. They moved constantly. We'd go months without hearing from her, and when we finally did, the news was always disturbing. Finally, when Arthur was just a little boy, Josiah disappeared. We begged Adelaide to come and live with us, but she refused. She always insisted our town was one of 'the bad places.' We sent her money, and your father checked on her whenever he could." Mrs. Johnson paused, and there was a sniffle that Thom didn't think was coming from Minnie anymore. "Arthur came here when Adelaide killed herself. She wrote a letter to me, telling me that she couldn't run anymore, asking me to take care of Arthur. So you see, he is family. And I won't fail him the way I failed his mother."

"What was she so scared of?"

"Scholarly nonsense. Josiah thought he'd discovered some ancient secret society that was controlling things across the world. Some silly Latin name — I can't remember. He was a very sick man, and he dragged Adelaide down with him. I thank God that Arthur is free of it all."

Charles caught his breath, and Thom put an arm around his thin shoulders to steady him. Whatever else was real, Mrs. Johnson was wrong about one thing: Arthur was not free of the Ladon Vitae.

None of them were.

FOURTEEN

CHARLES WENT FOR A WALK. Thom was too angry, worrying over what Arthur may or may not know, arguing with Minnie.

It made Charles tired. Frankly, he didn't care one whit about conspiracies or threats to his life. He was already dying, wasn't he?

By the time he reached the end of the lane he was out of breath, so he sat on the road and leaned back against a tree, the wildflowers growing madly up to his chest. Everything hurt. Sometimes he could ignore the pain, and sometimes the pain shut out the rest of the world.

He was unsurprised when a woman, tall and beautiful, stopped in front of him, a parasol shielding her from the sun.

"Hello, Charles," she said, smiling sweetly.

He squinted up at her. "Constance, I presume?"

She laughed, a lower sound than he'd expected. "Delighted to finally make your acquaintance. How are you?"

He shrugged. He didn't feel threatened or scared. In fact, right now, he felt nearly invincible. "Dying. You?"

She settled into the grass next to him, her skirts pooling out around her. "Not dying."

"I don't suppose you're going to be kidnapping me for nefarious purposes right now? There are a couple of things I'd like to do first, if you don't mind."

"By all means. We're not ready yet. But you're a remarkable child, aren't you?" She leaned closer, and Charles could see her face clearly. She looked young, face unlined, but there was something tired in her eyes. She reminded him of Alden in that way, that strange sense that her youth was a lie. "I wonder. I think I could offer you the moon and you'd politely turn me down." She sighed again, picking a flower and tucking it into his collar. "If we could all find the peace you have, the world would be a better place."

"It's very easy," Charles said, waving a hand wearily. His arm felt as though it weighed a million pounds. "Just realize that, no matter what you do, things are out of your control. Voilà! Peace!"

She took his hand and leaned close, then kissed his cheek. Her lips were cold against his skin. "Alas, dear one, I think I prefer turmoil and trauma and long life. See you soon."

He watched as she walked away, and then he closed his eyes to rest for the walk back to the boardinghouse. He had a feeling he didn't have much time left, and there were several very important things to do.

FIFTEEN

Minnie sat alone in the kitchen for some time after her mother, Thomas, and Charles had left. When Charles returned, she had her elbows on the table, resting her chin on her fists.

"Arthur's family history is the most dramatic story I've ever heard," she said, "and it doesn't delight me one bit. It makes my stomach hurt."

Charles nodded in sympathy. "Has Thom found him?"

Minnie shrugged, dropping her hands and slumping in her chair. She was having a hard time focusing enough to answer Charles's questions. Her mind was spinning. "I doubt it. Not if Arthur doesn't want to be found. And even if Thomas does corner him, Arthur won't say anything."

Arthur. Who is not my brother.

Minnie couldn't decide whether to laugh or cry now about the feelings she'd harbored since the day she'd first met him. She'd flirted with everyone, kissed any boy who'd wanted to kiss her, but it had never meant more than a warm friendship or a happy moment, because there was only ever Arthur in the back, front, and center of her mind.

I've hated myself so long for feeling this way. How can it be okay now?

She'd often daydreamed of getting this exact news, and how she'd throw herself into Arthur's arms upon receiving it. He'd realize he'd always been in love with her, too. There would be a lavish wedding on a dramatic cliff overlooking the ocean, and perhaps an epilogue of the sweetly spun decades to follow.

Loving Arthur was no longer a wicked-but-safe secret that she could never, ever tell. If she was allowed to love him, it also meant he was allowed to love her. Or not love her. And that second option made her feel so hollow and aching she didn't know what to do about it.

This was not a book, or a story. It was her life, and she knew perfectly well from the changes in Cora and the heavy, slow way her mother moved since her father died that life was not overly fond of delivering happy endings.

She looked up at Charles, who had gotten paler even in the short time they'd been at the boardinghouse. He seemed thinner as well, his cheekbones and jaw standing out in sharp relief. She realized with a start that he had wriggled into a place in her heart. None of her other flirtations had managed to get that far.

Perhaps she was merely a coward, but Charles was safe. She knew how a love story with him would end, unlike the ever-unknowable Arthur. She couldn't let anything happen to Charles. She wouldn't let anyone hurt him.

Including me.

"What are you going to do?" she asked.

"I'm not worried." He shrugged, toying with the teaspoon left on the table.

"But Arthur said they'd kill you!"

Charles leaned forward, giving her a conspiratorial grin. "What do I care? I'm already dying."

She felt his words like needles in her chest. "Don't say that."

"It's true. Thom pretends like it isn't, but I don't mind. At first I was angry, but then I figured, why spend my last few months bitter and angry over something I can't change? Besides, I have no regrets about coming here. This is the perfect summer."

His eyes sparked with so much life as he grinned at her that she couldn't, wouldn't accept that he would ever die. She stood so fast her chair clattered to the ground. Rounding the table, she kissed him on the cheek and pulled him into a hug. "I won't let you go anywhere. And neither will Thomas."

"Well, that's settled, then."

She could hear the teasing laughter in his voice, but she didn't care. If Arthur terrified her now, Charles was the most comforting thing in her life, and she loved him for it.

"I have something for you," he said.

Minnie released him, pulling her chair right next to his and sitting back down. "If it's a secret, I think for once I don't want it."

He laughed. "No secret. Here." He reached into his pocket and pulled out a locket. On a gold chain, twisted like a delicate rope, the pendant swung and glittered. It was oval, filigreed, the pattern accented by stones that Minnie was quite sure were diamonds. She had never seen a more beautiful necklace.

"It was my mother's," Charles said, lifting it over Minnie's head and pulling her hair free of the chain so the cool metal rested against her neck.

Her hand hovered just above it, afraid to touch something so beautiful and precious. "I can't take this."

"You aren't taking it. I'm giving it to you. My mother wanted me to be happy, and you make me happy. So I want you to have it."

She looked up at her friend, her eyes brimming with tears. She wouldn't let anything happen to him. She couldn't. And if Arthur wouldn't help keep Charles safe . . .

"I have something for you, too," she whispered.

"A secret?" he asked, voice still light, as though they were playing.

"Yes. A very big secret. One that's not mine to give."

He frowned, puzzled, just as Thomas burst back into the kitchen with a stormy glower. "I can't find him anywhere."

Minnie stood, holding out her hand for Charles. Her heart felt heavy with the sadness of hope and betrayal. "I think I know where we can get some answers."

She led them out the back door, stopping at the small gardening shed and taking a shovel. "You'll have to do it," she said, handing it to Thomas.

He looked at the shovel warily. "Do what?"

"Dig up Arthur's secrets." Her traitorous toes dragging, she led them to the trees behind the house, right to the spot where Arthur had buried his mysterious case on his first night here.

He'd always tried not to be seen. She'd *always* seen him.

And now, to protect Charles, she'd given up a secret she thought she'd forever carry out of love for Arthur. Thomas started digging, and Minnie realized whatever was there, she didn't want to know. Not this way.

She turned and went straight back to the house, passing Cora on the way.

"What are you doing?" Cora asked.

Minnie waved in the direction of the tree. "Go see for yourself."

Without waiting to find out what her sister did, Minnie stomped into the house. If she were Arthur and she didn't want to be found . . .

She took the back stairs, then opened a door in the hall to the narrow, hidden set of stairs that led to the attic. Bypassing Arthur's room, the only finished one up there, she turned and crawled through a narrow space into the open, empty expanse of the rest of the attic.

Arthur was leaning against the wall next to the window, profile illuminated.

Minnie's heart hurt her so much she didn't know what to do with it, other than pull it straight out and beg him to take it from her.

"You're not my brother," she whispered.

"Hmm?" Arthur looked up at her, his expression troubled and distant.

"Why did you let me think you were my brother?"

He was silent for so long she thought he wouldn't answer. She thought she caught a moment of hope, of joy in his face, but it was quickly replaced with sadness. Then, finally, he said, "It was easier."

"For who? It wasn't easier for me! All this time I've hated myself for how I feel about you! I've felt so wicked and so vile, and still I loved you! But it wasn't — it isn't — we could . . ." She trailed off, the air between them desperate and heavy with the words she wanted him to say.

"We can't."

"Is it Cora? Do you love Cora?"

He stood and walked over to her, so close she couldn't stand it, couldn't breathe.

"Of course I love her. Like I love you. And your mother. You three are all I have." His voice was calm, carefully paced and toned. "I can't love you like that."

Minnie took a step back, eyes narrowed. "You *can't*, or you *don't*?" The smallest twitch in expression shaped his eyes. It was a shift that only she, who had devoted so much time to studying him, would have caught.

"I don't," he whispered.

He was lying, and for some reason that hurt her more than if the words had been the truth.

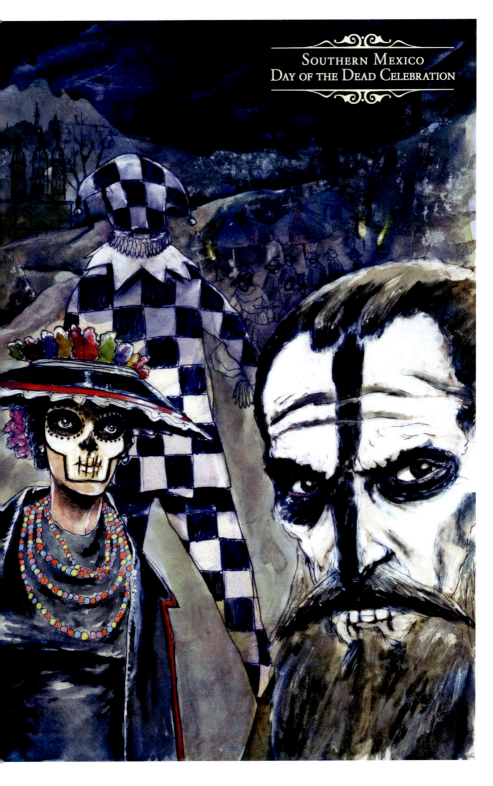

November 2, 1963

ORA PEERED DOWN AT THE CASE NOW SITTING ON THE FLOOR IN THOMAS AND CHARLES'S ROOM. It was wrong to be doing this, prying into Arthur's secrets. She would have liked nothing more than to ponder her relief at discovering he was not her half brother. But for some reason that information made him feel even more unknowable.

She was scared, and she hated that Arthur was part of what she was afraid of. There were too many other things to be frightened of without adding someone she trusted to the list. He would understand. Eventually.

So she wiped the remaining dirt of the case's grave on her apron and waited while Thomas fiddled with the latches.

Charles flopped onto his bed and closed his eyes, and for a moment Cora was more troubled by being in a room alone with the two boys than she was by betraying Arthur.

"We can leave the door open, if you'd like," Thomas said. His acknowledgment of her discomfort was enough to alleviate it, and she knelt next to him, smiling grimly.

The case popped open and they both looked up, locking gazes. Before she realized what she was doing, her fingers rested against his cheek. His eyes widened in surprise and she blushed, dropping her hand into the case and hastily pulling out the first item.

It was a portrait. The paint was oil, thick and textured, the weight of the portrait hinting at age. It had been torn and frayed along the edges, as though pulled roughly from a frame. Even though the paint was cracked and slightly warped, the image was instantly recognizable. Cora narrowed her eyes in disbelief. "Is that . . . ?"

Thomas leaned forward and let out a whispered epithet.

"Alden," she said, her stomach clenching as Thomas confirmed it with a nod.

"I'm really tired of that man," Charles said from the bed, his voice sleepy and unconcerned.

"Keep going," Cora said, setting the portrait carefully to the side and then wiping her fingers, which felt oily and stained with Alden's image.

Thomas pulled out a leather-bound notebook filled with loose papers. He cracked it open and Cora crawled to sit next to him. The writing was odd, sometimes gouged into the paper, sometimes running together to near illegibility as though the author feared he'd run out of time.

Page after page of it, Thomas flipping through them until he stopped on a list of names. "Here now," he whispered, then pulled a piece of paper out of his vest pocket, unfolding and smoothing it. "Looks like someone was keeping tabs on just what this Ladon Vitae was up to."

The names on the two lists frequently matched, but the book had far more details. Kidnapping, blackmail, conspiracies . . .

"Does that say *Napoleon*?" Thomas asked, squinting in disbelief at the book.

"Are they after him, too?" Charles shifted in bed, pulling a pillow over his head so his voice was muffled. "Someone ought to tell them he's quite dead."

"How do we fight this?" Thomas leaned back, fear and exhaustion written onto his face.

It hurt Cora to see him like that, to be unable to fix it. She needed to fix it. She looked back at the book, her eyes watering, fixed on the term *Blackmail* underlined twice next to a name she didn't recognize.

And then she had an idea.

Cora handed a stack of parcels to Annie O'Connell, who was making the weekly delivery to the post. "Thank you."

Annie nodded, turning her head to shrug the thanks off. She was pleasant and quiet and did her work well. It made Cora sad most of the time, seeing how easily the role she played to help her mother was filled by someone else. But right now she had plenty of other worries to fill her mind. Annie was welcome to the dusting.

She wanted to watch until Annie reached the end of the lane, but it was important not to draw attention to what she was doing until it was too late for anyone to stop it. She could work in secret, too. So Cora turned and went back inside, toward the sitting room where she could hear Thomas's restless playing.

She was nearly there when a voice behind her made her freeze.

"Excuse me," Alden said.

Cora turned, her expression carefully neutral. He couldn't know what she knew. "Yes?"

"I believe someone broke into my room."

"Have you spoken with my mother about it? She'll want to know so she can help rectify the situation."

He leaned closer, face above hers, and she resisted the urge to shrink away. She couldn't shake the image of the oil painting superimposed onto his actual features. She took a large, determined step backward, increasing the distance between them.

His mouth twisted into a smirk. "I haven't spoken to your mother, no. I thought perhaps you'd know something about it. Or maybe one of your friends."

"I assure you, sir, we hold ourselves to the strictest standards here. I can personally vouch for the staff. Perhaps during maid service some of your belongings were shifted. Is anything missing?"

"Nothing irreplaceable. Come with me; I'll do an inventory and you can take note." He held out his arm.

"I'll call for my mother."

Before she could move, he closed the distance between them, backing her into the wall. "I didn't ask for your mother, did I? You're a bright girl, Cora. Don't play at being dense."

Alden was grabbed from behind and shoved roughly away. Cora realized with a gasping relief that the piano music had stopped. Thomas moved in front of her, shielding her.

"Leave her alone," he said, his normally mellow voice a growl.

Alden seemed unperturbed. "Perhaps you are the one to talk to about the disturbance to my personal property."

Thomas didn't so much as flinch. "Perhaps I am. Whatever you and your friends think you can do to my family, you're wrong. I won't stand for it."

A note of glee entered Alden's voice. "You won't! How wonderful. But what do you know, really? Perhaps you found some words you don't understand. Or . . . a list of names."

"Whatever business you have with my father, you leave Charles and me out of it. If you so much as look at us the wrong way — and that includes Cora — I'll go straight to the police chief with a story so horrible he'll lock you up on the spot. And I promise my father's lawyers will make certain it's permanent."

"What are these threats for? We have no desire to harm you or your brother. Is that what has you so worked up?"

"I saw the list. My father's name, with sacrifice and blood debts."

Alden laughed. "This is why you need to ask questions before jumping to conclusions! You assumed the debt was your father's.

What if the debt is, in fact, mine? And my colleagues and I are working our hardest to come clear by helping your poor, sick brother?"

Cora frowned, peering around Thomas's shoulder. Alden's face was wide, his expression open.

"Doctors and medicine can do nothing, am I correct? Your brother is condemned to an early death. But there are things in this world that go beyond science, beyond the understanding of rational men. Your father knows about them. He helped us, once, and now begged us to do the same. That's why he sent you here, where we are gathering."

"Why wouldn't he have told us?" Thomas sounded unsure.

"Because he didn't want to get your hopes up if it didn't work. He has his doubts, but he said he was willing to try anything."

"What . . . kinds of things can you do?"

Alden pulled out his pocket watch, glancing at the time before clicking it shut. "These are not things for hallway conversations. Indeed, they are not things for conversations at all. You'll need to see it, I think, to truly understand. Then you can decide whether or not you want us to help Charles. We would never force it on you. Meet me at the boathouse on the northern pier in thirty minutes." He glanced at Cora. "And come alone. The debt is for your family only, and I'm already betraying covenants by speaking so openly to you."

Tipping his hat to Cora and nodding to Thomas, Alden turned and left the hall, whistling softly.

"What are you going to do?" Cora asked.

Thomas turned toward her, leaning against the wall and rubbing his face. "I don't know. I thought — well, we *could* have been wrong all along. After all, none of them have threatened Charles or me directly. And my father sent us here on purpose. He would never send us somewhere we wouldn't be safe. I wish I could just talk to him and get some answers, but he's out of the country again."

"Are you going to meet Alden?"

Thomas shrugged. "I don't see what other option I have."

"You don't really think he can help Charles, do you? Thomas, he frightens me. There's something not right about him."

"There's also something not right about my brother dying at fifteen. If there's some way — any way — to help him, I'll do it." Thomas's expression was intense, his voice heavy with emotion.

"They won't help him," Arthur said, melting out of the shadows beneath the stairway. "There's no help to be found with the Ladon Vitae."

"I'm sorry, since when are you the expert?"

Arthur's face darkened. "I know more than you."

"Well, you aren't telling, now, are you? Alden said he'd give me answers. I'm going to get them."

"These people are more dangerous than you can begin to imagine."

"Then stop whining about it and come along and see what their game is."

"How do you know?" Cora said.

Arthur froze, his eyes darting to her. "What?"

She couldn't quite meet his gaze. "How do you know how dangerous they are? What do you know, Arthur?" She wanted — *needed* — him to tell them the truth. How much did he know about what was in the case? Did he know more than what they found?

And why wouldn't he tell them, if it meant protecting people they cared about?

He cleared his throat, seemed to shrink back on himself. She knew he would lie before he opened his mouth. "They followed

Charles and Thomas here. Obviously they're organized and ill-intentioned."

She gave him a tiny nod, not trusting herself to speak. So he would continue to hide the truth. It made it bother her less to manipulate him, then. "But we don't know that for sure. If they could help Charles . . . And surely you don't want Thomas to go alone, if it's as dangerous as you seem to suspect."

Arthur's shoulders dropped, a defeated expression pulling at his face. "I promised my mother I'd be careful."

"We'll be careful," Thomas said, impatiently inching toward the door. "Besides, it's nothing to do with your mother."

Arthur stiffened and Cora went to him, taking his hand in hers. She wanted to give him another chance to be honest, to prove she was right to trust him. "My mother told Minnie. About your parents."

"You don't know anything about them," Arthur said softly, staring at the floor.

She did, though. She knew all about his father, could tell what kind of man he was from the ink he bled over hundreds of pages. Obsessive. Determined. Utterly focused on something bigger than himself, to the ultimate destruction of his entire family.

What had Arthur inherited from him?

Finally Arthur looked up, a burning intensity in his eyes that frightened Cora. Suddenly he seemed so much more than quiet, hidden Arthur. He had never before struck her as . . . dangerous. "Well, come on, then. You want your answers so desperately. Let's go get them."

Thomas's cut of a smile matched Arthur's expression. "All right. I have a couple of knives in my room. Cora, you stay here with Minnie and Charles. Keep together and don't leave the boardinghouse."

She nodded and, fretting, watched them head up the stairs.

The door to the piano room right next to her creaked open. Minnie and Charles peered out. "Is the coast clear?" Minnie asked.

Cora frowned. "Yes."

"Well, let's go! If we want to beat them all and have enough time to hide in the boathouse, we'll have to hurry!"

She grabbed Cora's hand, Charles on her other side, and ran out of the house. Cora wanted to protest, but couldn't find it in herself. She wanted to know, needed to, even, whether there were things stronger and stranger in this life than what she saw every day. She couldn't shake the feeling that the Ladon Vitae were more than just blackmailers and conspiracists. There were too many odd notes, too many images. If there really were other — *supernatural* — factors at play, perhaps then she'd have answers as to whether or not she really had contributed in some way to her father's death.

At the lane they saw Daniel going by with a horse and cart. "I'll be too tired to keep up this pace the whole way," Cora said, careful not to look at Charles so they could pretend it wasn't about him.

"Hey!" Minnie shouted. "Daniel! Give us a lift to town, would you?"

He stopped and let them catch up, waiting just long enough for them to scramble into the back before clicking his tongue for the horse to go on. "I'm going to the station. Where to?"

"The north pier will be fine, thank you." Cora watched nervously behind them. But they were fast enough that she didn't see Arthur and Thomas come out of the boardinghouse.

When Daniel dropped them off, Cora had second thoughts. "We really oughtn't do this. Alden said for Thomas to come alone."

Minnie scowled, pulling the door to the dilapidated boathouse open and checking inside. "Thomas is already bringing Arthur. And no one will know we're here. Besides, it's not really Thomas and Arthur's business, anyway, is it? It's Charles's."

Charles nodded reassuringly at Cora. "That's right. If anyone should be let in on the magical healing secrets of the Ladon Vitae, it's me."

Minnie walked in, complaining about the stench of fish. Cora hesitated, looking at Charles. "You don't really think there's anything they can do to help you, do you?"

Charles shrugged. "No, I don't. I'm mad they're yanking Thom's chain, is all. He doesn't deserve any more disappointment. He's a good brother. The best brother." He held Cora's eyes in a way that felt significant, as though trying to feel whether or not she understood just how valued Thomas was.

Cora nodded solemnly, a winsome smile tugging on her lips. "He is."

Charles seemed to relax, as though a question had been answered. "I'm glad we agree. He's going to need a lot of help when I'm gone. Now, come on. We can't let them see us!"

Cora followed him inside. The dim contours of the room began to sharpen, settling into focus. A few stacked crates crowded against them, and a single grimy window set high in the wall opposite begrudgingly let some light in. The floor extended halfway across the small building, where it ended at the rock wall of the pier. Mild waves slapped lazily, sliding back and forth under the gate that opened to allow a single small boat in.

"Over here," Minnie whispered, waving them toward the back. Several crates were stacked high enough for them to slip behind and be out of view, as long as they pressed against each other.

Cora wondered how long they would have to wait, but it was only a few minutes before Thomas and Arthur could be heard, arguing softly. The door opened again and the boys' muffled footsteps filled the silence. Cora was certain her heart was beating so loudly they'd be able to hear it. Sneaking and spying were Minnie's pastimes, not hers, and she hated the fear of discovery combined with the guilt of deception.

"He's not here yet," Thomas said. "We're early, I think."

"Right on time, actually," Alden answered. A small scratching sound was followed by a flickering yellow light throwing their hiding place into even deeper shadow. "I must thank you for being so obliging, Thomas. And for bringing the Liska brat with you. One generation must go as another, I suppose."

"What are you going to show us?" Thomas asked, wariness straining his voice.

"I'm going to show you what happens when you think an ant can tell a god what to do." Glass shattered, and the room was filled with the acrid scent of kerosene and smoke. "Good-bye, little ants." The door slammed.

An impact rattled the walls of the boathouse, followed by another. "He's barred it!" Arthur shouted.

"Arthur? Thomas?" Cora peered out from behind the crates. Arthur's eyes widened in terror as he saw her, Minnie, and Charles. He and Thomas ran toward them, but the line of flame had reached a barrel propped against the wall.

A popping sound was followed by a low boom, and then the entire boathouse was bathed in brilliant, biting orange light.

OCTOBER 8, 1967

SEVENTEEN

ARTHUR BLINKED, HIS HEAD POUNDING. Where was he? What was happening?

A violent shout next to him brought him to his senses. Minnie had taken off her overshirt and was using it to smother the flames licking at Thomas's trousers. The wall with the door out was entirely consumed by fire, and the air was already thick with smoke.

Arthur sat up, dizzy, and put his hand to his head to find it covered in blood.

Must have hit it in the explosion.

". . . Arthur! Look at me!" Cora's face swam into view in front of him, sharpening his focus entirely. "We have to get out of here."

"Are you okay?" Minnie asked Thomas, who was crawling toward where Charles sat against the far wall, eyes wide and breath shallow.

"I'm fine! I'll be fine. We've got to get out!"

"The door is blocked," Arthur said, sluggishly trying to sort his thoughts. They needed to leave through the door, but the door was blocked.

Minnie hurried across the narrow strip of wood that skirted the water and led to the two gate-like doors that opened onto the ocean to let boats in or out. She shook them, but Arthur could see the padlock firmly in place. "We'll have to swim for it!" Minnie said.

"What if he's out there watching for us?" Cora asked.

"Dive deep. Stay under as long as you can. After you get under the gate, go left behind the boathouse. We can hang on out there until we see whether it's clear to go. And be careful of the waves. If it's high tide, they'll be pounding harder."

Arthur felt he should be the one saying what to do, figuring out how to get them out of here. Minnie needed *his* help. But she was calm and in control, while he could barely think straight. When had she become this way?

Another popping sound was followed by a burst of light and heat so intense Arthur could smell the hair on his arms charring.

"I'll get Charles!" Thomas said. He pulled Charles up, putting his hands on his face and pulling him close, whispering something. Charles nodded, and then, Thomas's arm around his waist, they dove into the water.

"Come on!" Minnie said, jumping off by the gate and treading water, waiting. Cora dove straight down, and before Arthur could call out she was under the gate and out of the boathouse. Minnie followed.

Arthur was alone in the burning building.

And he could not swim.

He climbed on top of a crate, choking on the smoke, and pulled desperately at the long, narrow window. It was sealed shut.

The flames found another barrel and, with a noise that left his ears deafened, exploded. The force of it sent Arthur off the box and straight into the water.

He choked, flailing, trying to force his head above water. Fire and smoke and water each pulled at his senses, disorienting him. After only a few seconds his head went under and he knew he wouldn't get it up again.

A hand grabbed his, tugging him. His head broke the surface, and he found Minnie next to him. "Hold on to my shoulders and kick your legs. I won't let you drown."

Arthur shook his head, more terrified of the cold depths than he was of the licking flames.

"Arthur," Minnie said, demanding that his eyes focus only on her. "I will not let you go. Take a deep breath, and then we're swimming out of here."

He nodded. She turned around and let him put his hands on her shoulders. He squeezed her, too tightly, and took as deep a breath as he could in the smoke-choked air.

And then they were in the freezing dark of the ocean water. He kicked erratically, smashing his knees into Minnie's legs, but she pulled them deeper, under the gate. Arthur saw light playing above them and tried to steer her up, but she swam harder, still going deeper, turning them and pulling herself along the mussel-covered rock foundation of the building.

When Arthur thought his lungs would burst, Minnie abruptly changed course, pushing straight up and gasping for breath along with him. She immediately guided his hands to the foundation of the building.

He clung to it, filled with fear and relief and also a deep shame. He hadn't protected Cora and Minnie at all. He'd nearly gotten them killed. And Minnie had been the one to save his life.

"Everyone okay?" Minnie said, breathing hard.

"Yes," Cora answered. She was next to Thomas and Charles. Charles was shivering violently in the cold water, his lips blue. The sun was nearly down, and the waves slammed them mercilessly against the foundation.

Arthur looked up to see the flames eating through the wood on this side of the building.

Minnie followed his gaze. "It doesn't matter if he's waiting or not — we have to get away from this building. I'll swim ahead and check."

"Wait, you can't —" Arthur started, but she had already disappeared under the water. Every second was agony until she popped back up again, on the far side of the boathouse.

"Come on! I don't see him anywhere. You can go along the side of the building, and then it's only a few feet to the pier."

Thomas guided Charles, helping him along, followed by Cora. Minnie swam back to Arthur, clinging to the side next to him and going slowly. Arthur noticed dark, wet smears where her hands had touched.

"You're bleeding!"

She shrugged, grimacing. "The mussels. They're nasty sharp beasts."

This, of all things, filled him with so much rage he was certain he would kill Alden with his bare hands if he saw him again, no matter the consequence. But now he had to focus on survival. He followed Minnie around the edge and let her grab his waist and, in a jumble of flailing limbs, help him to the pier.

They pulled themselves out of the water and collapsed next to the others, shivering and out of breath. The heat from the building next to them was almost pleasant, but they needed to get away, and fast.

"Daniel's at the station," Cora said in a breathless pant. "We need to tell him what Alden did."

Arthur shook his head, trying to clear it of the smoke, water, and pain. "Daniel, then," he said, his voice coming out far lower and angrier than normal. Cora put her arm around Minnie; Thomas supported Charles; and Arthur walked behind all of them like a shadow.

He didn't want to hold that spot anymore, he found.

Arthur was grateful for the shield of twilight around them. Otherwise their appearance would have attracted more stares and curiosity than he could handle at the moment. It was nearly full dark by the time they reached the sheriff's office.

Cora and Minnie charged ahead, moving toward the door, but Arthur heard voices inside.

"Wait," he hissed. He moved against the still-warm bricks of the building and motioned for the others to do the same. Crouching next to the propped-open window, they heard Daniel.

And Alden.

". . . burning right now. I saw them as I was walking by, and when I turned around at the end of the pier, the building was on fire."

There was a clatter of chairs, and then Daniel sprinted out of the building, followed by the sheriff. They ran in the direction opposite Arthur and the others, heading for the small fire station on the next street.

Arthur looked up to see Alden standing on the steps to the office, looking down and smiling at them. He tipped his hat, then walked at a leisurely pace back toward the boardinghouse.

"Oh, no," Cora whispered. "We can't go to Daniel now."

"We'll tell the truth! He'll believe us!" Minnie wrung her hands, the jacket Charles had given her slipping off one shoulder.

"Minnie," Thomas said, shaking his head. "He already thought we lied to him about Mary. And who would you believe: the well-dressed, wealthy summer visitor, or five soaking-wet, smoke-covered kids? Arthur's bleeding from his head. Your hands are cut to pieces. I have burns on my legs. We look guilty."

"But who can we tell? Who will help us?"

"No one," Arthur said, his heart as dark and heavy as the night around them. He had hoped that the day would never come. It was time to discover his father's secrets and pray that they would offer him a way out, a way to save those he loved.

The secrets that had killed his family were his only hope for saving Minnie and Cora.

An unforeseen setback has consumed an [...] amount of my time and made any leads I had turn cold.

I thought I was so close, but they have eyes everywhere — as you well know.

That said, I am hoping all has remained well with you and your family while I was... away.

Before I continue pursuing my primary targets, our other targets have grown bold in my absence.

I am about to attempt to remedy that, which will continue to aid our other mutual goal.

I will visit soon.

Be ready...

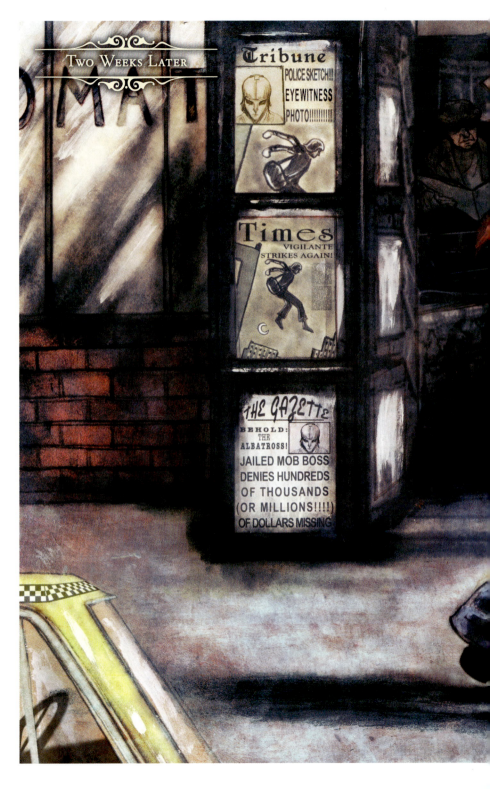

EIGHTEEN

THOM PACED NERVOUSLY, ALWAYS KEEPING HIS BROTHER IN HIS PERIPHERAL VISION. Charles couldn't stop shivering, lying on the sofa with three quilts over him. Cora and Minnie had met them in the small library, hair still wet but clothes changed. Arthur had disappeared somewhere — Thom wasn't sure where. It was getting late — soon Mrs. Johnson would chide them for not being in bed — but none of them were anywhere near being able to sleep. They wouldn't be able to until Alden was gone.

"I still say we should tell Mama," Minnie said. She looked small and pale, sitting on the sofa with her legs tucked up beneath herself. She toyed with a heavy gold locket around her neck that seemed familiar. "She'll know what to do."

Thom shook his head. "If we talk to your mother, Alden'll just tell her that we were in his room, going through his things." He didn't say what he thought next, which was if the man was willing to burn two boys to death, he certainly would have nothing against harming Mrs. Johnson if she got in his way.

"What about —" Cora was interrupted by the door being shoved open with such force it dented the wall.

"What have you done with it?" Arthur shouted, as loud and as physically *here* as Thom had ever seen him. Before Thom could get away, Arthur had rushed across the room, grabbing him by the collar and shoving him against a bookshelf. The wood dug into Thom's back.

"Arthur! Stop it!" Cora shouted, hurrying to pull him off Thom. Arthur wouldn't move.

"I know it was you. I want the case back. Now."

Thom met the other boy's gaze with a steady one of his own. "It's in my room. You can get it whenever you want. I won't apologize; we needed information, and you had it."

Arthur slammed him against the bookshelf again, the air whooshing from Thom's lungs in a painful burst. "Did you take anything? Is it all there?"

Clenching his jaw, Thom shook his head. Arthur's fist slammed against his stomach, making him double over in pain.

"Stop it!" Minnie screamed. "It's my fault! I told them where you'd buried it." She ducked under Arthur's arms, smashing herself between him and Thom, voice laden with tears. "I'm sorry. I'm so sorry. But they are going to hurt Charles."

When Arthur dropped Thom's collar, Thom slid to the ground, stomach still sharp with pain. He was getting rather tired of being attacked tonight. The next person to hit him would be hit back, no matter who it was.

"I don't care if they hurt Charles," Arthur said, his voice now the quiet one Thom was used to.

Thom stood with a growl, anger boiling to the surface. It was only Cora's hand on his chest that kept him away from the other boy. Of course Arthur didn't care — he'd made that abundantly clear. But Charles was *everything* Thom cared about. In that moment Thom knew that, because of Arthur's desire to protect the girls, he was as much a threat as Alden.

Minnie stepped forward, trying to wrap her arms around Arthur's waist. He moved away from her, his eyes cold.

"I care if they hurt him," she said, her shoulders shaking.

"We're leaving." Arthur grabbed Minnie's wrist and turned to Cora. "Right now. We can't stay here any longer — it's not safe."

"Are you mad?" Cora asked. "We can't leave!"

"I'll make you. If I have to tie you both up and throw you in a trunk, I'll make you, so help me."

"And then what?" Charles glared at him. "How are you going to take care of the two of them? Where will you get money? Where will you stay? How is running away with them any safer than staying here?"

Minnie twisted her arm, pulling free. Her huge eyes impossibly sad, she shook her head, then went and sat next to Charles on the sofa. Thom watched, glad that in the midst of all this, Minnie was choosing his brother. He could see the pain in Arthur's face, and it filled him with a vicious happiness.

You have no one, Arthur.

"I can't leave," she said.

"Neither can I." Cora dropped her hand from Thom's chest and, to his shock, took his own in hers. Her fingers were long and soft in his.

"We'll protect them," Thom said. He looked from Cora to Minnie, finally settling his gaze on Charles. "All of them. With or without your help."

Arthur left the room without a word.

Early that morning, so early the sky was still blushing away the remnants of night, Thom made his way to Arthur's attic room, case in hand. He knocked on the door, but it swung open under his fist.

"Arthur? Listen, I wanted to say sorry, and ask —" Thom stopped short on the threshold of the room. Sitting on Arthur's bed, holding a stack of letters, was the witch.

"Hello," she said, smiling dreamily at him, her eyes flitting around like a butterfly, alighting on his for only a second before flying away again. "I came to see the Liska boy, but he's not here." Her lip jutted out in a pout.

"Oh. I'm sorry." Thom immediately felt like a fool. Here was the witch — Mary — whom he knew was involved with Alden and Constance, which meant she was probably part of the Ladon Vitae. She had obviously snuck into the house in the middle of the night doing who knows what, and Thom was *apologizing* to her?

"Listen," he said, trying to sound firm and menacing. "I want to know what this is all about. I know you're part of them, that secret society. Who are you people? And what do you have against Charles?"

Mary shuffled the stack of letters, pulling some out and stroking her finger along them. "Hmm? Who's Charles?"

"My brother!"

"I had a brother once. Brothers are horrible, aren't they? He used to do the most awful things to tease me. I would do anything to see him again." She sighed, a soul-weary sound, and set the letters back down, carefully tucking a picture into the ribbon.

Thom scowled in frustration. "Yes, but what do you want with *my* brother?"

"I don't want anything with him. I don't want anything at all in the whole world." She stood, the hem of her nightgown-like dress dragging across the floor as she walked toward him. He wanted to back up. There was something unnerving in the way she was finally looking at him, something strange about her eyes that he couldn't figure out. If she were a melody, she'd be discordant.

Her tongue darted out to wet her cracked lips. "Except an ending. Oh, how I ache for an ending. Would you give us one?" She cocked her head, considering him.

"If you help me keep my brother safe, I'll do whatever I can for you."

She nodded slowly, finally looking away from him. He felt as though it was easier to breathe. "Hmm. Who does your father love more?"

"What?"

"Which would hurt worse — being the son loved so much he is worthy of sacrifice, or being the son who's spared because he is the lesser?" She raised a hand and rested it on Thom's cheek. He flinched, but she didn't seem to notice. "I think the latter, but you'll have to tell me."

Thom swallowed hard. A sacrifice. Constance had spoken of that, and it was on the list next to his father's name, too. "He loves Charles more," Thom whispered. "He always has." It hurt something deep inside him to finally say it out loud, to admit to this stranger what he had always pretended not to know.

She nodded, patting his cheek. "Then Charles is the offering."

"Should we run?"

She drifted past him, lingering at the top of the stairs. "There isn't enough time."

"I'll fight him. Alden. I'll kill him if it means keeping my brother safe."

She turned toward him, a smile splitting her face in two, eyes bright with delight. "You should! You absolutely should. I thought it would be the Liska boy, but you might do as well." Laughing, she picked her way lightly down the stairs.

"So that's the answer? Kill Alden?"

"No, silly. Kill us *all*," she said just as she disappeared from view.

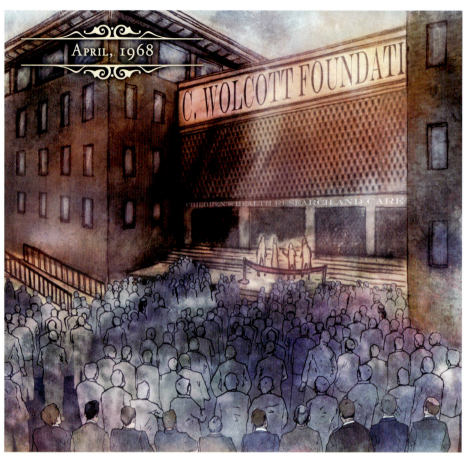

APRIL, 1968

C. WOLCOTT FOUNDATI

CHILDREN'S HEALTH RESEARCH AND CARE

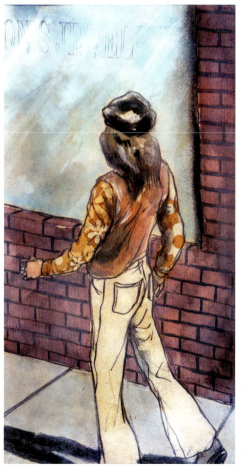

CHARLES SIPPED HIS TEA ON THE FRONT PORCH AND WATCHED AS A CROOKED MAN, OBSCURED BY A LENGTHY BEARD, SCUTTLED UP THE WALK, DECAPITATING FLOWERS WITH HIS UNUSED CANE.

"Afternoon," Charles said, nodding.

The man looked up, startled. When he spoke, his mouth twisted in a way that echoed the sense of crookedness woven throughout his body. "Afternoon."

"You'll be here to see Alden?"

The man paused, leaning against the porch railing. Charles could smell him this close, and he smelled of mothballs and garlic so strongly the tea lost all its appeal.

"And how did you know that?"

Charles shrugged. "You have the same eyes. Too old and too young at once."

The bearded man's smile grew and he tapped the side of his nose with one heavily knuckled finger. "Clever boy."

Charles leaned back against the pillows propped behind him in the rocker. He had figured some of the story out, reading Arthur's father's notes while Cora and Thom had plotted. Alden, Constance, this man — they liked being part of something secret and powerful. Everything they did, then, would naturally further this power. His father was wealthy and influential. Whether they'd helped him get there or merely taken advantage once he was, it didn't really matter. Every member of their group would do whatever they had to in order to keep their secrets and their power.

Well, except for Mary. She was the cog that his machine-oriented mind could not solve. Why would they include a woman so obviously out of her mind? Maybe she was someone important, after all.

But leaving Mary aside, he still couldn't figure out what their goal here was. If his father owed them money, surely it would have been simpler to kidnap him days ago. If they wanted to scare him into doing something for them, a threat made far more sense than locking Thom in a burning building.

Until that had happened, Charles hadn't been bothered — indeed, he had been entertained and enjoyed Thom's frantic attentions focused elsewhere. Now he was quietly seething over these people running around in his life, setting strange things in motion, hurting people he cared about.

He was angry, and being angry made him tired. "You know, you could simply tell me what's going on. All of this cloak-and-dagger nonsense wears a body out."

The man stood straight, tugging on the coarse ends of his black beard. "Ah, but where would be the fun in that? We need our diversions, too. Your body may get worn out, but ours merely get bored." He leaned forward, a cold gleam in his eyes making Charles scared for the first time. "Would you like to see a magic trick?"

The door opened and Alden, his hair perfectly oiled, stepped out. "Not now," he said, not so much as looking in Charles's direction. Charles was glad for that, because he knew his fear of Alden was written all over his face. The point of being out here was to *look* exposed, but with Alden so close Charles felt perilously, truly exposed.

Shrugging his regrets, the bearded man winked at Charles and followed Alden off the porch and onto the lane where they walked toward town.

Charles shivered in spite of the afternoon heat. He had decided that whatever this Ladon Vitae was planning, he really did not want to find out how they worked. It was one thing to come to terms with dying a natural, if early, death. Another to face it in a burning building, to watch it threaten the people he cared about most in the world.

Few things scared him anymore, but Alden filled him with a terror bigger than he had ever known, because Alden had found the only remaining things that could hurt Charles: Thom, Minnie, and Cora.

He leaned to the side and tapped three times against the window to the library.

Immediately Thom, Minnie, and Cora were outside. "Where are they headed?" Thom asked.

"Toward town."

He nodded, and Charles noticed an odd bulge beneath his vest. "What have you got there?"

Thom avoided his eyes, but Minnie gasped, turning to Cora. "You didn't!"

Cora glared at her. "I did, and you'll keep your mouth shut about it."

A movement in the corner of his vision caught Charles's eye, and he had just enough time to see Arthur, melting between trees, already following Alden and the bearded man.

"Arthur's beaten us!" he said, standing and hurrying down the steps.

"No, Charles, you stay here." Thom grabbed his elbow, trying to turn him back toward the boardinghouse.

"And leave me unprotected and alone? That's *precisely* what they have in mind." Charles thought no such thing, but he was not staying here.

"Come on, we're going to lose him!" Minnie ran ahead, the ribbons from her hat trailing behind her.

"Blast that girl," Cora muttered, taking Charles's arm and going as fast as she dared.

"Everyone follows my lead," Thom said when they caught up to Minnie. At every bend he slowed and peered cautiously ahead. "We only want to see who he is meeting with and where. Then we go to the sheriff and demand he listen to us. My father's name isn't worthless, and even if they don't believe us outright, I doubt this Ladon Vitae group wants to be noticed. And if the sheriff doesn't scare them off . . ."

He trailed off darkly, his hand drifting to his vest.

Charles did not like the bulk in Thom's vest. It made the aching in his chest sharper than ever. Thom was going to get himself in trouble. That's why Charles needed to come, though every part of his body was screaming in agony, begging him to lie down right here on the road.

They were as stealthy as they could be, following two men in broad daylight through a summer resort town. When they nearly knocked Arthur down as he slid out from a shadowed stoop, they were all shocked that Minnie was the first — and loudest — to curse in surprise.

"Go home," Arthur hissed.

"Make me," Minnie responded, glaring at him with an intensity he'd never seen.

Charles felt suddenly, painfully lonely.

"We're losing them." Cora pushed past, hurrying down the street with Charles on her arm. He wished she'd walk with a little less determined purpose.

"There! Into the same teahouse as before!" Thom nodded in grim triumph. "Let's go get the sheriff."

They turned and, Arthur and Minnie quietly arguing in the rear, made their way to the sheriff's office. Cora stomped up the stairs, pushing open the door without knocking. A man stood with his back to them, and Cora exclaimed in relief.

"Daniel! Oh, good. We need your help."

Daniel turned around, and Cora screamed in horror.

Where his irises should have been were blank white orbs, his face an expressionless imitation of a man's. He lifted a gun and, without blinking, pointed it directly at Thom.

Arthur slammed into Thom, knocking him out of the way as a bang and the scent of gunpowder assailed Charles's senses.

"Run!" Arthur shouted, pulling Thom up and dragging him toward the door. Daniel lurched toward them, his movements stiff and awkward as though he wasn't quite in control of his muscles.

Cora grabbed Charles roughly by the arm and they tripped down the stairs, bursting onto the street outside. "The church!" Minnie shouted, turning and sprinting down the sidewalk, elbowing a surprised and angry older woman out of the way.

Charles and Cora followed. Thom, glancing back, glared darkly. "You go! Arthur and I will try to draw him off."

Before Charles could protest, Cora had tugged him after Minnie, and they were running along toward her. She darted through crowds and sidewalk stalls, heedless of the gasps of indignation that followed her.

Charles wanted to help Thom.

He wanted to protect the girls.

But he could do neither because he couldn't breathe —

He couldn't, he couldn't, he couldn't breathe.

"Oh, Charles!" Cora cried out as he slumped against a wooden vegetable cart and slid to the ground, gasping for the air that would not fill his lungs, clutching at his chest as though he could tear the pain in his heart out.

Bright spots filled his vision as the edges of it dimmed, but before it faded to black he was lifted up as he heard Alden say in an oil-slick voice, "That's all right, ma'am. I'll take care of the boy. Come along, Cora. There's a good girl."

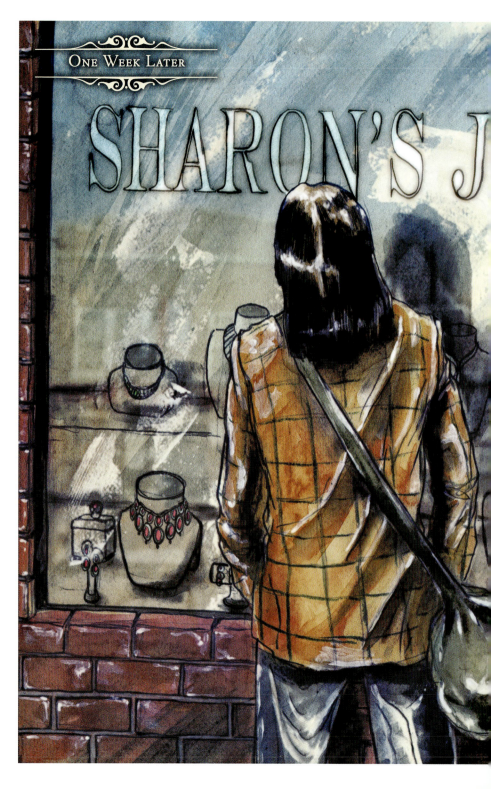

TWENTY

Minnie wouldn't wait in the church. She ran back along the sidewalk, retracing her route.

Where had the others gone?

Her panic rising with every second, she searched desperately. Cora. Charles. Thomas. Arthur.

No one! Where had they gone?

A hand came down heavily on her shoulder, another over her mouth as she was yanked into the narrow alley between the chemist's shop and the post office. Whoever had her held her squeezed against his chest, grasping her tightly around the waist and pinning her arms at her side.

"Well now," a voice, heavy with the scent of garlic, breathed in her ear. "I've caught one, too. I think it's my turn to choose a prize. I've seen you with the boys. Kisses as free as spring rain. You won't mind." He wheezed a laugh and Minnie felt a coarse beard scratching at the bare skin at the base of her neck.

She stomped on his foot as hard as she could, and, when his arm loosened, she grabbed the knife from under her skirt and turned.

She'd misjudged the space between them. The blade slid into his chest with a sickeningly wet sound.

"Oh," Minnie said, her voice soft and calm in spite of the horrible disconnect from reality she felt.

The bearded man looked down, his own eyes open wide in surprise.

Minnie pulled on the knife — it gave more resistance than she would have expected — and it came free with a spurt of dark blood.

The bearded man looked at her.

He smiled.

She turned and ran, the bloody knife still clutched in her fist. She didn't know what to do. All she could think of was the soft, wet give of his body beneath her knife, and the way he'd said, "I've caught one, too."

Too.

She was back at the church, pacing the steps, before she knew it. She kept repeating their faces — Cora, Arthur, Thomas, Charles — wondering who was gone.

She wondered if she'd just killed a man.

She wondered if she cared.

Wiping the knife on her dress, she put it back in the makeshift sheath against her leg. If something had happened to anyone she loved, she wouldn't care if she'd killed him. She would never care. She would do it again.

"Minnie!"

Her heart bright with hope that hurt like pain, she looked up to see Arthur, her Arthur, running toward her, followed by Thomas. And then she looked past them and saw no one, and the hope crashed into terror and despair.

"They aren't with you," she said.

"Where is my brother?" Thomas demanded, putting his hands on her shoulders and shaking her. "Where is he?" His face was shadowed in the dimming evening light. There was already a large bruise blooming on his cheekbone.

Minnie ignored him, looking to Arthur, pleading silently with him to make it not true. He would produce Cora and Charles. He would have already saved them.

Minnie saw the gun was now in Arthur's hand, his eyes fixed on a point to the left of her.

For a brief moment she wanted to sink to the ground in

despair, to give up, to be anyone but herself. This was not a story she wanted to tell. It was not the story she wanted to be in. She had dreamed so many times of danger and intrigue, weaving imaginings around herself so tightly she could no longer see reality.

Had she created this horror, then? Had she wished it upon all of them?

Steeling her shoulders, she pushed Thomas's hands away. "If I knew, I wouldn't be here! They've been taken. We have to get them back!"

"Why is there blood on your skirt?" Arthur said, a note of unaccustomed panic in his voice.

"I'm not hurt." She glared at him and then at Thomas, daring either of them to question her further. They didn't, just as she didn't question why Arthur held the gun.

"The teahouse," Thomas said, twitching, already moving in that direction. "They meet at the teahouse!"

"They won't be there." Minnie knew for certain. That had been the trap, the lure. Whatever Alden and his friends had planned, they were not deeds for teahouses and towns, certainly. "Arthur, I need you to tell me everything you know about the Ladon Vitae."

His voice came out a dead whisper. "No."

"We don't have time for secrets! They have my sister!"

"I know!" He choked on the words, looking at her with wild fear in his eyes. "But if I tell you, if you know, then you'll be tainted, too. I can't let that happen, Minnie. I have to keep you safe."

She held up her hand, still stained with blood. "We're not safe anymore. None of us. It's too late for that."

"I can't lose you. I love you."

The words charged through her like lightning, a physical sensation she felt to her fingertips. She stood on her tiptoes and pulled his face down, meeting his lips with her own in a kiss so longed and hoped for it was more an act of desperation than passion.

He looked dazed as she pulled back, still holding his face so that he couldn't break eye contact. She locked him there and didn't let him go. "You will *never* lose me."

Finally he nodded, swallowing painfully. "We need somewhere old. If this is one of the places they visit, they'll have a history here and they'll use it. There are certain places they consider powerful, and they come back to them over and over again. That's one of the ways my father tracked them."

Thomas cleared his throat. Minnie had forgotten he was right there. She didn't care. He nodded toward the church. "Isn't this one of the oldest buildings?"

Arthur shook his head. "Older. We're talking centuries."

"But the town isn't that old!"

They both looked toward Minnie. She ran through every structure, every building, but they were right. Nothing was older than one hundred years. Nothing had the kind of deep-rooted history that Arthur was talking about. It would need to predate the town, predate the first settlers, even.

And then she knew.

"The caves!" she said, immediately breaking into a run. "They were used for rituals!"

"I thought that was just a story!" Arthur said, running to catch up so that he and Thomas flanked her.

"Everything is just a story. Stories are the only things that matter."

Minnie prayed silently that they would make it in time to rewrite the ending.

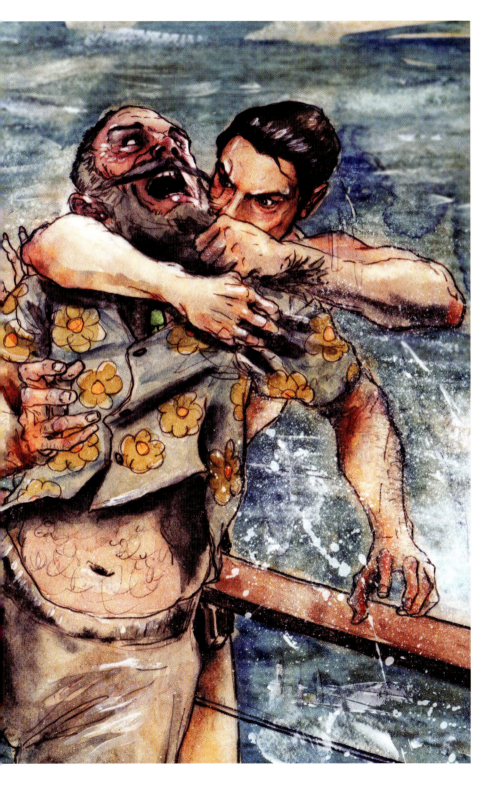

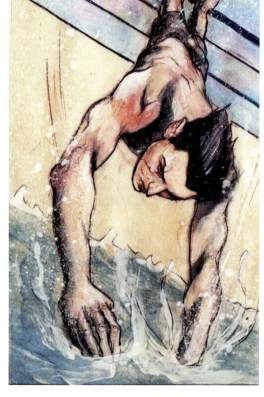

TWENTY-ONE

THE LOW TONES OF AN ARGUMENT ECHOED AROUND CORA. They were punctuated by the slow, maddeningly arrhythmic dripping of water from the cave ceiling into pools around them. She sat on the ground, unforgiving shards of rocks beneath her, with Charles's head cradled in her lap. He was starting to get some color back, and his breathing seemed less labored, but she wanted to get him to a doctor right away.

Unfortunately, their way was blocked. They were being kept by Alden, Mary, the woman she assumed to be Constance, and several other people she didn't recognize but who seemed vaguely familiar, as though she'd passed them on the street. Alden stood nearest to the way out, his tall frame almost pushing his head against the cavern roof. Around him, carved into the rock, were designs Cora had mistaken for water grooves, but that she could now see were symbols and letters, painstakingly created to blend in.

Mary, ignoring the heated exchange between Alden and Constance, drifted toward Cora, trailing her finger along the rocks.

She looked down and smiled tenderly at Charles. "Don't worry," she said.

"Of course I'm worried," Cora hissed, too angry to be frightened of the woman who had plagued her nightmares for years. "Charles will die if we don't get him help."

"Oh, he's going to die anyway. Didn't you know?" Mary looked up, her wide eyes crinkled with sympathy.

"I know he's sick, but it doesn't mean he has to die!"

"No, child, he's going to die tonight." Sighing heavily, Mary sat down next to them, then put her head next to Charles's in Cora's lap. Cora wanted to shove it away, but some mad, lonely fierceness in Mary's face stopped her.

Mary reached out and stroked Charles's hair. "Lucky, sweet boy."

"Did I kill my father?" Cora whispered, staring at Mary.

Mary shifted so she looked up into Cora's face. She frowned. "Did you? I thought you were a nice girl."

"That day I fell out of your tree. You told me death was chasing me. I ran home and then my father died. Did it — did death follow me and take him instead?"

"It doesn't work that way."

"You mean, you didn't send death after me?"

Mary laughed, the sound ringing through the cave. "If I could command death, none of us would be here."

Cora let out a shaking breath. It wasn't her fault, then. She hadn't brought tragedy to her home. It had found them all on its own. For some reason random pain was more comforting to her than pain that could be traced to a definite cause.

"Thank you," she said, nodding at Mary.

"Mary, darling, come away from there." Alden glared reproachfully at her, and Cora had the sudden urge to draw Mary closer. She put her arm around Mary's fragile shoulders.

"See, that is my point exactly." Constance held a handkerchief to her nose as though the entire scene offended her every sensibility, including smell. "You have demonstrated an inability to choose wisely when it comes to your pets. The girl never should have been involved. She's a local; she'll be missed. This is neither the time nor the place for games you have never played well."

"Hear, hear," a tall, exotic-looking man said, nodding toward Constance. "We should be deciding how best to expand our influence."

Alden sneered. "Is that wise? I should think we'd want to be quiet for the next few years, given our elements in play in Europe. Am I the only one who thinks long-term?"

"And that's why you've kidnapped another girl? Long-term thinking?" Constance's tone was biting, and it made Cora's blood run cold.

An enraged shriek shot through the air and echoed along the stone walls until it surrounded them.

"Minnie," Cora whispered in despair and frustration.

A percussive bang left her ears ringing.

"Nobody move!" Thomas shouted.

"Charles!" Cora whispered, clutching him tighter. "They're here!"

Constance's smile shifted from biting to delighted. "By all means, come in!" she said, waving coquettishly and moving to the side in a swish of her skirts. "Do join us."

His face a mixture of fear and determination, Thomas walked into the chamber, his eyes immediately alighting on Cora and then Charles. With a cry, he ran to them, dropping to his knees and feeling for Charles's pulse.

"I'm fine," Charles muttered, eyelids fluttering. "Sleeping."

"Sleeping!" Mary echoed in a singsong tone.

Thom looked at Cora and she nodded, trying to convey that she was fine, too. He reached up and smoothed the hair back from her forehead, and she leaned into his fingers, closing her eyes and, for a brief moment, letting herself feel safe.

Minnie walked in next, a short knife from the kitchen clutched in her fist. She let out a small sob when she saw Cora, but did not run to her. Instead, she put herself between Cora and Alden, knife held at the ready.

And finally Arthur, as pale as she'd ever seen him, expressionless and holding the gun, came in. He leveled it at Alden's chest and pulled the trigger.

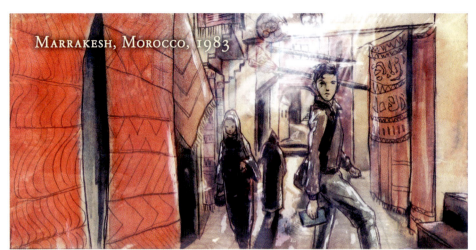

MARRAKESH, MOROCCO, 1983

OKINAWA, JAPAN, 1988

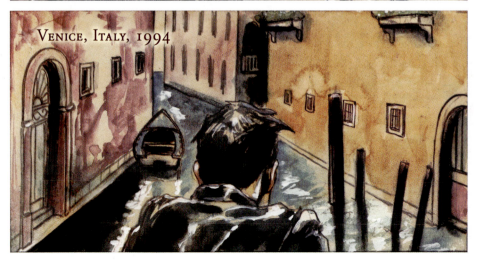

VENICE, ITALY, 1994

JODHPUR, INDIA, 1999

BERKELEY, CALIFORNIA, 2009

THE REPORT OF THE GUN ECHOED AROUND THE SMALL CHAMBER. Alden looked down at his chest, frowning. "Move the cage," he growled. The other Ladon Vitae, except Constance, melted back into the shadows of the cavernous passageway.

Constance laughed, drawing Arthur's attention. He leveled the gun at her, but he didn't think he could shoot a woman. "How very like your father you are, Arthur!" she said.

"What do you mean?" He moved toward Cora and Minnie, keeping the gun pointed at the members of the Ladon Vitae. This was not going as he'd expected. He'd thought they'd run, or they'd fight, or something.

There was an odd scraping noise coming from another branch of the cave system, along with some grunts, but he couldn't see what the others were doing, and he wouldn't leave Alden and Constance to go find out.

Constance tapped her chin as though deep in thought. "I seem to recall the elder Liska doing the same thing to Alden. Amusing."

Grimacing, Alden pulled out a handkerchief and dabbed it at the blood. "It is less amusing to be on the receiving end of the bullet." Arthur had shot him in the chest. He shouldn't still be breathing, much less standing there cleaning himself up.

Constance waved dismissively. "Of course. Now, if you've got that quite out of your system." She raised an eyebrow and looked pointedly at the gun.

Utterly mystified and at a loss as for what to do next, Arthur lowered his hand.

The bearded man stomped into the cavern, glaring.

"And where have you been?" Alden asked, putting away his ruined handkerchief.

"Had to change my shirt." The bearded man leered at Minnie. "It had blood on it."

"That seems to be a common theme tonight."

Minnie raised her knife, trembling. "I — you — I stabbed you in the chest. And Arthur shot you! How is this —"

Constance clapped her hands together. "I do love it when they try to wrap their little minds around it all. The moment they realize what they are up against, and their hopes come crashing down. You can see a bit of their soul shriveling then and there. You were right, Alden — this *is* a fun addition to our gathering."

"Can't die, can't die," Mary sang, her tune mournful and eerie in the cave.

"Yes, *thank you*, Mary." Constance sighed impatiently. "Do be a dear and go wait outside with the carriages." Mary stood and twirled, bare feet spinning slowly along the ground, as she left the caverns.

Arthur staggered back as though he had been shot himself. Were these the *same* people his father had traced through the ages? The portraits, then, didn't just look old — they really were that ancient? Had his father figured it out? Had he known the true secret of the Ladon Vitae?

"What happened to my father?" he asked. Here, at last, were his answers, and dread and rage warred within him.

"This," Alden said, snarling, as he raised a gun and pointed it at Arthur's chest.

"Stop!" Thomas roared, filling the cave with his voice. "If he dies, you all go down!"

Alden pursed his lips in annoyance, but nodded for Thomas to continue.

"We stole your papers. Lists, names, information. We took some of Arthur's father's notes, too. I've sent them to a contact somewhere far from here. If any of us — *any of us* — are harmed or die in an unnatural manner, the information goes straight to a newspaper I know will publish them."

"Blackmail," Cora said, her voice soft but her eyes hard.

Arthur could not take his eyes off Alden, off the man, the *monster*, who had killed his father. His father, who had also tried and failed to end this reign of terror.

"Well now," Constance murmured. "This complicates things."

"Let's kill them and have done with it," the bearded man grumbled. "What's an article in a paper?"

Constance put a hand on his shoulder, preventing him from walking forward. "Yes, but think this through. Certainly no lasting harm will come from it, but it will draw eyes to our secrets. We'll have to lie low for a while. Years, maybe decades."

Decades. It spun in Arthur's head, impossible but true.

"So? We've done it before."

"We have some rather large plans in the works in Europe right now, if you'll recall." Her gaze on the bearded man was sharp, and he winced under it. "I, for one, would hate to let things slip out of our hands when we have been building this for so long."

"What about the boy?" Alden asked, nodding toward Charles, who had managed to sit up. "We still need a blood sacrifice for our *friend*. And Wolcott owes us his debt."

Constance glanced at the brothers. "You do understand now what happened?"

"Our father," Thomas spat, "made some sort of deal with you, and Charles was the sacrifice. But I won't let you touch him."

"I think that settles our account with Mr. Wolcott. The price was one son, and he's now effectively lost both. We can find the blood we need elsewhere, in a less . . . complicated manner."

"And they get away free and clear," Alden said, matching the intensity of Arthur's glare. Arthur trembled with his desire, his need to hurt this man. To kill him.

"Hardly. They'll spend the rest of their lives looking over their shoulders and having nightmares." Constance paused as though pretending to be in thought, then clucked disapprovingly. "Oh, I forgot. You wanted the girl for a new plaything. Well, we all must choose what is best for the group."

The cutting edge of her smile hinted that she and Alden had a history longer and more complicated than Arthur could ever understand. But he didn't care about her. He didn't care about any of them. He wanted Alden.

"Very well." Alden let out a heavy breath, but did not lower his gun. "Constance, see to the loading of the cage." She nodded and left with a swish of her skirts, followed by the bearded man, who was still grumbling under his breath.

Alden half-turned to follow them, then paused. "Still, we ought to give these children something to remember us by."

Before Arthur could raise his gun, Alden had shoved him out of the way and grabbed Minnie. He jerked her head back, whispering in her ear and holding his beetle pendant against her forehead. Her voice cut off mid-scream as her shoulders slumped and her gaze turned toward the ground.

"Get away from her!" Arthur roared, his heart in his throat. Alden held Minnie in front of his body as a shield, the gun in Arthur's hand feeling more worthless than ever.

"She's unharmed," Alden said, a cruel laugh shaping his words. "And certainly not dead, so our end of the bargain is upheld."

Arthur rushed to Minnie as Alden backed out of the cave. He expected her to fall, but she stood, completely still, where she was.

"Minnie?" he asked, his voice trembling. She didn't look up.

Taking her chin, he tilted her face toward his own.

Her eyes were blank white orbs, with no soul or fire behind them.

Minnie was gone.

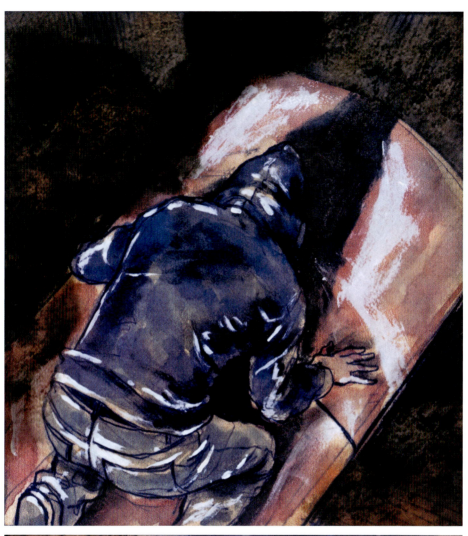

TWENTY-THREE

INNIE! Minnie!" Cora screamed her name over and over, shaking her sister by the shoulders as though she could wake her up.

Thom couldn't look at either of them. He felt this was his fault, that he had somehow traded Charles's fate for Minnie's. And while he couldn't be sorry about saving his brother, he couldn't help but wonder: How many months of life did Charles have left? It wasn't a fair trade, not in any world. Minnie and Cora should never have been part of this. The rest of them had their chains they couldn't escape — two fathers, both damning their sons to collisions with the Ladon Vitae in different ways.

But Minnie? Dancing, laughing, storytelling Minnie?

The air had been sucked out of the cave along with Minnie's soul, and Thom wondered if he'd ever be able to breathe properly again.

"Please," Charles whispered. "Please, you have to fix this." Thom looked at him, but found Charles with his head bowed. The same brother who had never once bemoaned his own fate, never once pled on his own behalf for divine intervention, was praying for the girl he loved.

Cora looked up, her expression ragged and hollow. "How did you fix Daniel? He stopped chasing you, right? Maybe it wears off!"

Arthur sank to the ground, holding his head in his hands, pulling at his hair. "I shot him."

"You *what*?"

"He wouldn't stop. I shot him in the leg, and he still wouldn't stop. He was crawling after us when we lost him."

The blood drained from Cora's face, and she trembled as she pulled Minnie against her chest. Minnie didn't resist. She didn't do anything.

"We'll go get them," Thom said, feeling a fierce, reckless courage take root in his chest. "Alden. We'll do whatever we have to do to him to make him fix this."

"Everyone is so sad," a sleepy voice said from behind Thom. He whipped around to find Mary, plucking at her thin dress and biting her lip.

"You!" He rushed forward and grabbed the woman, pulling her by her bony elbow into the room and shoving her against the rock wall. "Tell us how we can fix this!"

She blinked, unperturbed by his use of force. It was that more than anything that filled him with shame, made him let her go.

"*You* can't," she said, black eyes nearly as blank as Minnie's.

Cora's sob tore out of her throat, the sound going straight through Thom like a knife.

"Tell me how I can kill him," Arthur said, standing, his face an unreadable mask.

Mary's eyes lit at that, something burning deep within them. "That is better. What would you give up to do that?"

"Anything!" Thom shouted. Maybe if they killed Alden, whatever spell he put on Minnie would be broken.

Mary's smile grew, her expression dreamy. "I've been waiting. So long. I tried to do it myself, a few times, but he always knew. And I loved him, once. I forget when. And why."

"How can we kill him?" Arthur pressed, leaning toward Mary, his shoulder against Thom's.

"You must *become* him. Or me. I'm so very tired. I'd like to sleep. Sleep and not dream." Her gaze drifted away, eyes focusing on something they couldn't see. "It's never been the right time, because then no one would be here to hate them. But I can trust you to do that."

Arthur grabbed her shoulder, forcing her attention back on them. "Tell us."

"Alden thinks he's the only one the boy will talk to. But the boy and I, we're kindred spirits. A cage of iron" — she paused and gestured at her body — "or a cage of unbreakable flesh. Both trapped. And so he talked to me. He gave it to me." Her expression lost its dreamy quality and became something clever and sharp. She reached into a pocket sewn onto the front of her dress and pulled out a scrap of paper, indecipherable writing in a dark brown, rusty-looking stain on the paper.

Blood.

"What is that?" Thom whispered.

"This is the way to the path. The unending path. I stepped onto it once, and I wish more than anything I could find a way off. Will you make that step?" She looked at him, her gaze piercing, as though she would see into Thom's very soul.

"You mean . . . that could make us immortal?"

"Only one. I'll only change one of you. And then you have to help me."

"What about Minnie?" Cora asked.

"If you'll help me sleep?"

Cora nodded solemnly. "We will. I promise."

Mary reached around her neck and pulled on a string. Out of the front of her dress came a pendant, the dark green beetle. "We made them, you know. So none of us could hurt the others." She stroked the pendant. "But there are so many ways to hurt someone, aren't there?"

Humming off-tune, she walked past Thom and Arthur, and slipped the necklace over Minnie's head.

Thom held his breath, watching, and at first he thought he was only seeing what he wanted to, but no — there! Minnie's dark eyes came through as the white slowly faded away.

She took a deep, shuddering breath as though coming up from beneath water. "Arthur?" she asked, eyes finding him first.

"Oh, Minnie!" Cora pulled her into a hug, crying into her sister's hair. "Minnie, you're back!"

"Thank you," Charles gasped. Thom's heart broke to see how pale he was, how his lips were tinged in blue, but how happy he managed to look at the same time. His prayers had actually been answered.

And that's when Thom realized — *his brother didn't have to die.*

"Do it to Charles," he said.

"Hmm?" Mary asked, pulling the necklace back over Minnie's head and tucking it into her own pocket.

"Charles. Do the spell on him. It'll fix him, right? He won't die."

Charles's frown matched Mary's. She looked at him, considering. "I don't think he's right for it."

Standing shakily, Charles walked over to take Minnie's hand, drawing her close. Arthur hung back from all of them, eyes half-hooded, lost in thought.

"I don't think I want it," Charles said.

"Charles," Thom hissed, pulling him away from Minnie. "Don't be daft. You won't die!"

Charles shrugged. "Look at Mary. Does she seem happy to be immortal?"

"That's not the point!"

"You saw what being involved with this group made our father do. Why would I want to have anything to do with them?"

"But —"

"He's not the right one," Mary said, standing with her back to them and tracing her finger along the carvings etched into the wall. "He's not angry."

Thom looked to the girls, but Cora was focused entirely on Minnie, and Minnie was staring at Arthur with a frightened look on her face.

Thom turned to Arthur, who met his eyes. He walked to the other boy, leaned in as close as he could to Arthur's ear. "We trick her. I'll tell her it's for me. We get the spell and then we do it on Charles."

"Charles doesn't want it."

"I don't care what he thinks he wants! If I can save my brother, I'm going to!"

Arthur leaned back, then shook his head. "No."

Desperate, Thom turned to Minnie. He knew Charles was in love with her. If anyone could convince him to take a chance, to accept this altered life, she could. "Minnie." He begged her with his eyes, and she looked from him to Charles. "Please."

"Would it be so bad?" she whispered, putting her hand on Charles's cheek. "It couldn't change who you are. You're not your father."

Charles looked uncertain. Thom seized on the moment. "I'll do it," he said, holding out his hand to Mary. "Give me the spell."

"No," Arthur said, his voice cold and determined. "Don't give it to him, Mary. He wants it for Charles."

"What are you doing?" Thom turned to him, horrified.

"I can't let you waste it."

"*Waste* it? My brother's life is a *waste*?"

"It has to be used to take down the Ladon Vitae. They have to be stopped. They have to pay. Charles won't do that. I'm sorry, but I won't let him take this."

"Who says it's your choice?" Thom moved to grab Arthur's collar, but Arthur was faster, ducking under Thom's arm and bringing his fist up into Thom's stomach. The air left his lungs in a painful whoosh.

"It has to be me." Arthur walked past Thom toward Mary, whose face was alight with a beatific joy.

"No," Thom growled, grabbing Arthur's arm and throwing him to the ground. Arthur's face bounced off of the sharp rocks there, a crescent cut over his eye already beginning to bleed freely.

"I'm sorry," Arthur whispered, then kicked out at Thom's knee. Lights exploded in Thom's vision as the pain burst through his body.

TWENTY-FOUR

Thomas!" Cora cried, dropping to the ground next to him. Thomas clutched his knee in agony. He wouldn't be able to walk, not on his own.

And he wouldn't be able to stop Arthur.

Mary's hungry look was tinged with sadness as she watched them all.

"Give it to me," Arthur said, standing up and wiping his eyebrow free of the blood that was stinging his eye.

"Arthur, no." Minnie put herself between Arthur and Mary, taking his hands in hers. He tried to avoid her eyes but she wouldn't let him, forcing him to look at her. "No. You heard her — you can't come back. Not if you choose this. We'll lose you."

His voice came out far calmer than he thought it would. Looking at Minnie, he realized just how much he would be giving up to devote himself to this new path. "I have to. They killed my father. I can't let them get away. And it's the only way to know you'll be safe. I won't let anyone hurt you, not again."

"*You're* hurting me," she whispered.

Now his voice caught in his throat, a solid lump of pain lodged there.

She went on. "You'll have to leave us. All of us. Who knows when you'll come back?"

"I'll hunt them down and finish this. As fast as I can."

Minnie's eyes glistened with tears. "But . . . what if the person who comes back isn't you anymore? Arthur, you're not just sacrificing Charles's only chance at living. You're sacrificing your own soul. You're going into the dark and I'm scared — I'm so scared you'll never be able to come home. It can't be worth it."

Arthur leaned toward her. He wanted to take her in his arms, to kiss her, to tell her that he would choose her. But he couldn't. The rage and pain burned too bleakly in his heart. The Ladon Vitae had taken everything from him. And now he would lose Minnie. But he'd make them pay. He'd end this.

"It's worth it to me," he said.

Minnie stumbled back as though Arthur had struck her.

"Arthur," Cora started, but Minnie shook her head.

"No," she said. "Leave him. He isn't choosing us."

Cora and Charles stood, balancing Thomas between them. He hopped as well as he could, and when they passed near Arthur, Thomas muttered, "I hope your immortal life is hell."

Mary watched them leave, but put a hand out to stop Minnie. Arthur didn't know what to say, couldn't say anything. He had to create a world in which Minnie was safe. He had to create a world in which his father's murder and his mother's madness were avenged. He wished, more than anything, he could be like Charles, so that simply living with what he had, simply loving Minnie, could be enough.

"Poor child," Mary cooed. "It is the sharpest, deepest cut of all, isn't it? I wouldn't wish love on anyone. It carves a hole in you that can never be filled."

"He'll be alone," Minnie said, not looking at Arthur. He didn't know whether it hurt more to have her avoid his eyes or force him to see the pain there. "I would have waited for him. Forever."

Mary put her face down, her forehead against Minnie's. Arthur couldn't stand the aching to go to her, not anymore, so he turned and faced the wall of the cavern. Now that it was quiet, the wind whispered secrets, soft sibilant noises just short of words.

When he let himself look, Minnie was gone.

Mary passed a hand over her eyes, her shoulders slumped wearily. "You must do something for me, after."

"Anything."

"Take me out on the ocean. Weigh me down with rocks, and drop me into the depths."

Arthur narrowed his eyes. "Why?"

"If I cannot die, at least I can finally sleep. Cold, dark, empty sleep, until the end comes."

He started to shake his head, but she looked at him with such hope he found he couldn't deny her this last terrible request.

"At least my destruction is one of peace and rest. Unlike yours." Smiling, Mary pulled the scarab beetle pendant out of her pocket and draped it over Arthur's head. "Are you ready?"

He swallowed, then nodded.

He was.

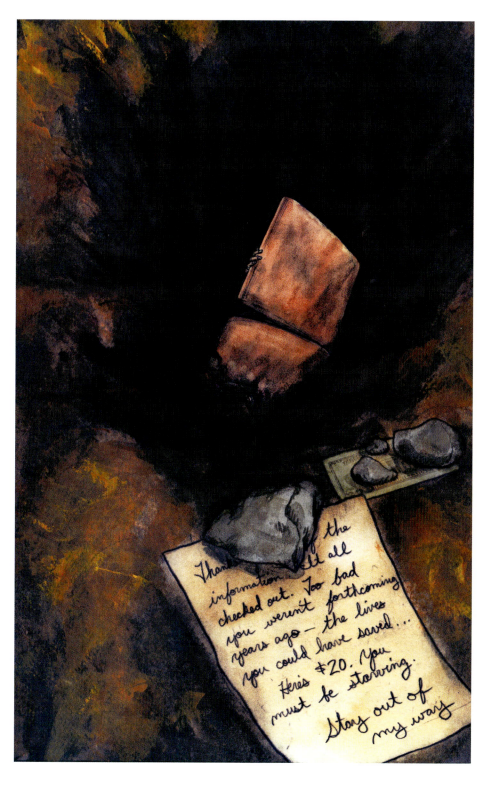

TWENTY-FIVE

THE WAVES LAPPED AT THE ROCKS, NEARLY REACHING THEIR FEET WHERE THEY HAD STOPPED. Thom couldn't go any farther on his leg, and Charles needed to rest as well. Thom sat, heavy with the weight of failure.

"It's over," Charles said.

"Oh, Charles." Thom hung his head. "I'm so sorry. If I'd been faster, or cleverer, or —"

He was rewarded with a small rock bouncing off his shoulder. "Don't be daft. I meant it in a good way. As good as can be, given the circumstances. We're free."

"Not all of us," Minnie whispered, standing apart from the other three, her back to them and her toes in the water.

"That was his choice." Cora took Thom's hand in her own. She radiated both sadness and peace, and Thom found her skin infinitely comforting. "He could have come with us. But he chose to keep his fate tied to them. And I'm very sorry for it." She squeezed Thom's fingers. "What will you do now?"

"We aren't going home, if that's what you mean." He couldn't think on his father without feeling sick to his stomach. Whatever the Ladon Vitae had done, whatever horrible webs they had woven around him, it didn't matter. In the end, he hadn't fought for his sons. Thom would never go back to him. Neither he nor Charles would so much as write to the man to let him know of their escape.

"Stay with us. At the boardinghouse. Mother will let you stay on as long as you want. And now that Arth — well, we could use two smart men around the place."

Charles nodded solemnly. "I'm happy to do it, but you'll have to put out an advertisement for the second smart-man role. I don't know where you'll find another."

Cora laughed, and with the sound some of the pressure released from Thom's chest. They were alive, and safe, and free. They still had each other.

Charles would die. He knew that. But while he was alive, he would be happy, and that was enough for him.

Thom was already calculating how long an appropriate courtship would last before he could make Cora his bride.

Cora would say yes, happily, finally freed from the burden of guilt that had pulled on her for so long.

Minnie watched the ocean, where, at the place where the caves jutted out into the water, a small, dark craft had launched into the water. She would make Charles's last months filled with light and joy. She would make Cora take herself less seriously. She would encourage the romance between her sister and Thomas. And she would wait for the return of a person she never expected to see again.

When she turned back to the others, she smiled, and they were all so relieved that none of them saw the dark, empty void that had taken up residence in her soul, the choices before her. Mary had been right. Loving someone really was the worst sort of agony.

And she could never stop.

"At least we have each other," Charles said, holding his hand out to Minnie. She took it, taking Cora's in her other. Linked thus, they all thought the same thing, but no one spoke it:

Arthur had no one now.

CHICAGO,
18 Days Ago

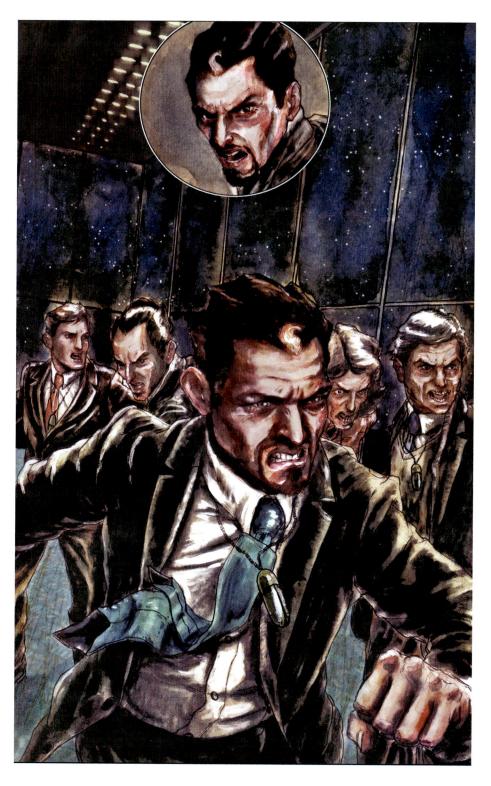

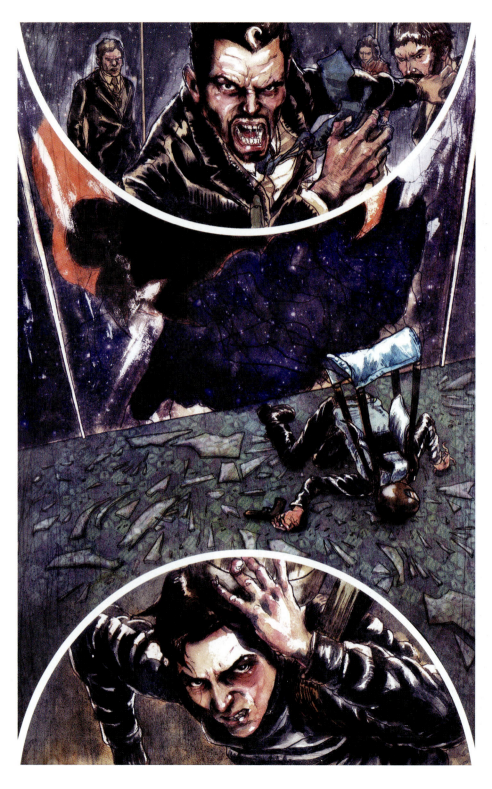

TWENTY-SIX

H E DIDN'T HAVE MUCH TIME BEFORE THE OTHERS CAME
BACK. It wasn't dawn yet, but the hired carriage waited
for him outside.

He traced his hand along the contours of his attic room, knowing that he was about to leave it behind forever.

He couldn't account for how he felt — for how it had felt
when Mary had said the words and changed him. In part it seemed
as though he were trapped in a waking dream. Everything around
him was slow and oddly lit, as though anticipating the sunrise.
He was deeply aware of the beating of his own heart and, in a
strange way he'd never before noticed, the very pull of the earth
beneath him.

He had miles to go yet. Miles and miles.

Reaching up, he put a finger tenderly to his eye, but the cut
was already healed. Only a scar remained. It struck him as appropriate, that his last moments as a mortal would mark him forever.

Gathering his father's things, he packed them into his traveling case. Paintings of various members. A list of contacts they had,
including Mr. Wolcott. A list of locations his father was certain
the Ladon Vitae visited ritualistically. It was a starting point, but
if the Ladon Vitae only met every ten years, he might never be in
the right place at the right time.

It wasn't enough to go on, and a sense of despair pulled at him.
How could he end something unending?

He fell back onto his pillow and heard an odd rustling. Reaching beneath it, he found Mary's forgotten letters. The return

address was in a hand he now knew to be Alden's. A flat in London. It was a starting point, and he took it as a sign he was on the right trail.

Tucked into the letters, though, was something new. A photo of —

Arthur sat up. A photo of Minnie, perfectly preserved from the beginning of summer. Her face was serene, placid; not even holding still for the exposure could dampen the light in her eyes.

He had done that all on his own.

He turned it around to find a scrawling note, written in a hand that could only be Mary's:

Fear the men, not the monster. Free the demon and free us all.

The demon. Mary had whispered about it as he slowly rowed her out to the ocean. Arthur thought she was just ranting, but now he wondered if she wasn't telling him how to destroy his immortal enemies.

"None of us are what we seem," she had said. "Least of all the demon. Poor sweet thing, ancient nightmare caught, then caged in flesh and blood for all of us to live off. You'd look right at him and never know. I wonder if I'm a monster inside, too? What does my skin hide?" She'd scratched at her arm until it bled, then sighed and continued wrapping chains around her ankles. "So hard to find. But you'll release us all, won't you?"

Arthur shuddered, thinking of Mary's idea of release. He owed it to her — to everyone — to figure out the clues, to chase Alden down, to find this demon and free it. To end the Ladon Vitae once and for all.

The carriage was waiting. Closing his case, he climbed out the window. If he walked past the rooms where he had had a home for the first time in so many years, where he had been happy, he didn't think he could go through with it.

This was best. He would leave Minnie, Cora, and Mrs. Johnson. He would leave Thomas and Charles and trust them to take care of the girls in his absence. He would leave.

It was not lost on him that he was leaving the house the same way he had arrived: alone and afraid.

But this time he knew what he would do with the path he was on.

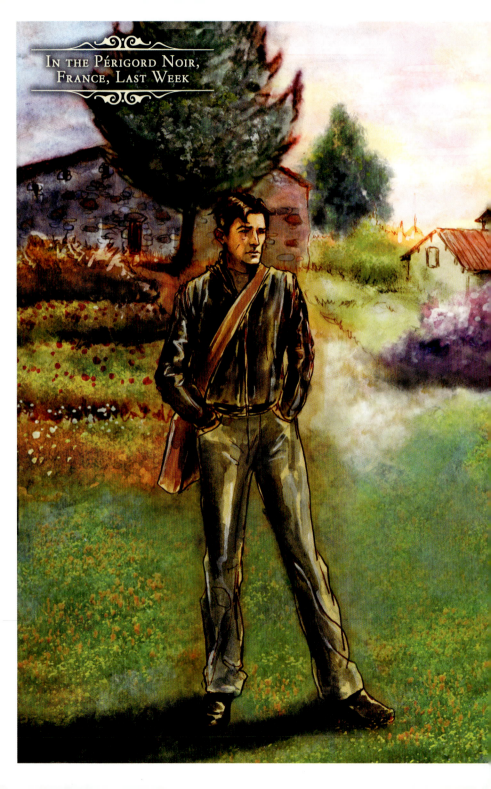

TWENTY-SEVEN

ORA AND THOMAS FOUND IN EACH OTHER SOMEONE TO BOTH TAKE CARE OF AND BE TAKEN CARE OF BY, AND THEY WERE HAPPY AND CONTENT AND HAD RIDICU-LOUSLY FAT BABIES WHOSE LAUGHTER WAS LIKE LIQUID JOY. Thomas became a musician, and, after the boardinghouse burned down, their family moved to New York. But they returned, staying every summer with Minnie like the terrible tourists they'd always looked down on.

Charles lingered on for longer than any doctors predicted. Minnie stayed by his side and was with him for his last cheery breath, taken just after making a joke at his brother's expense. He was mourned the way he lived: with gratitude for the time he'd had.

Minnie was left alone. But she held on to a secret, one she hadn't shared with even her sister.

Mary had given her a choice.

That night in the cavern, Mary had pulled her close and whispered of the pain and horror of love. And then she had given Minnie the spell, the words that would let her live forever so that Arthur wouldn't have to go on his dark path alone.

But Minnie didn't know what to choose. By the time Charles was gone and Minnie realized she could not live her life knowing Arthur would be alone forever, she had no way of finding him. Arthur had disappeared, and with him the clues to tracking the Ladon Vitae.

In her heart of hearts, though, Minnie knew she had promised Arthur something. She would wait for him.

Forever.

And so, on a quiet night, in the solitude of the trees by the witch's house she now claimed as her own, Minnie alone stepped out of the path of time and onto the lonely path of immortality to wait for Arthur to come home.

Minnie waited. She watched her sister and brother-in-law grow old and gray, and then watched her nieces and nephews do the same. She stopped attending funerals, because they became too many. She became very adept at forging official documents and new birth certificates, and the town that had always harbored a small share of magic turned a blind eye to their new witch.

And while she waited, she wrote the stories of her town, the stories of her childhood, the stories of her long, long years. She sent the books out into the world along with her hopes that Arthur would find them and know he wasn't alone.

She didn't just write. She read. Minnie couldn't track the Ladon Vitae, but she learned enough to know that if someone could find their source of power, then maybe the curse of immortality would be broken and the Ladon Vitae destroyed. Every eternal day, every endless winter and infinite summer, she hoped that Arthur was safe. And with vicious focus she prayed that he would find what he hunted.

And then one day, the Earth started turning again. She felt it in the sudden painful thump of her heart, the way the dust motes seemed to swirl instead of hang lifeless on the air, the way the ocean no longer felt like an ageless companion, but rather a sleeping giant she could never comprehend.

She knew, then, that Arthur had done it. He'd destroyed the Ladon Vitae's power and returned all of them to mortality. And with the mortal breath bursting in her lungs, she laughed and raced to the top of her house to watch for Arthur walking up the hill.

He didn't come.

All her long, aching years of waiting, all Arthur's suffering and hunting, and still they were alone. Sometimes she wondered whether she ought to leave, give up on the lifetimes spent hoping. But whenever a storm raged over the sea, she watched it. She remembered his eyes, and she knew she had made the right choice.

Find me, Arthur, she would whisper.

I'll wait forever.

Come home.

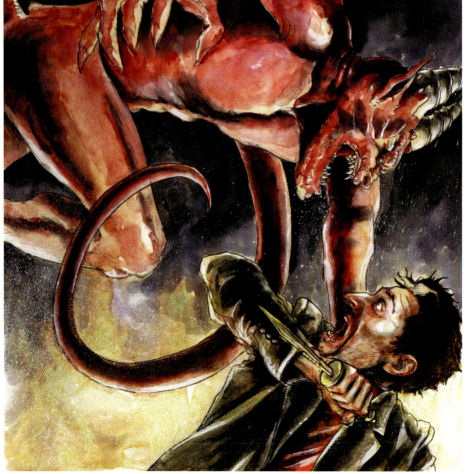

·THE END·

ACKNOWLEDGMENTS

From Jim Di Bartolo

I will never be able to begin any sort of summation of thanks without thinking first of my lovely, talented wife, Laini. We've built a life I couldn't have imagined possible. Thank you for everything. My in-house art-director and partner in all things meaningful to me. Life with you is a magical dream.

For Clementine. You cuddly little comedian. Thank you for letting me scribble various thumbnails into your sketchbooks when we're drawing together. I can't wait to read your inevitable books.

Boundless thanks to Kiersten White for creating such lyrical, lovely, and creepily wondrous text chapters. Your words here are true artistry, and your ability to create such whole, unique characters is breathtaking. I'll never forget reading those first chapters from you as they e-zoomed my way and floored me. Wow, lady! Thank you, too, for our friendship before and throughout this collaboration. It has been a treat!

For Jane Putch. Agent-and-friend extraordinaire. What a life-improving force and influence you have been in my life and the life of my family. Thank you for suggesting I approach other authors to collaborate — and for encouraging me to pursue stories that I would have fun drawing and painting. This has been a DREAM project because of you. Thank you for always believing in me, and for everything you've done for Kiersten and me with this book. You are a gift!

To David Levithan. For early and ever-present praise-filled

enthusiasm, and for your dedication to this book. You excitedly let us try something different than the norm. For that and your countless other separate achievements, you sir, are awesome, and an inspiration. Also, the music you've introduced into my life has fueled dozens of pages herein. Cheers!

To Chris Stengel for hours and hours of thought and care in book design and collaboration. Many thanks for you and your talent!

To Mama and my late Papa. For their encouragement and support. And for my foundation. Anything good within my core is because of you both. Love you.

From Kiersten White

First thanks, always, to my wonderful husband, Noah. I would have waited forever for you, but I'm so glad I didn't have to. Also to our beautiful children, Elena, Jonah, and Ezra, simply for existing in such an infinitely delightful manner.

So many thanks to Jim Di Bartolo. I wanted something new, and this exceeded all of my creative expectations. Thank you for thinking of me, for being so amazing to work with, and for being such an incredibly gifted artist and storyteller. One word: ears.

Special thanks to the combined talents of Michelle Wolfson and Jane Putch, our intrepid literary agents, who took this hybrid weirdo of a book and found the perfect home for it.

And of course to our editor, David Levithan, who is brilliant and insightful and was willing to take a chance. Thank you for seeing our vision for this project and helping us every step of the way to getting there. No one would have done a better job.

To everyone at Scholastic, thank you for making our book a reality. From design to copyedits to marketing, we couldn't have asked for a better team.

And finally, thank you to our readers for bringing their own minds and magic to the pages.